FRANCIE
=== AND ===
THE BOYS

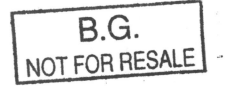

FRANCIE
=== AND ===
THE BOYS

BY

MEREDITH
DANEMAN

**Delacorte
Press**

Published by
Delacorte Press
Bantam Doubleday Dell Publishing Group, Inc.
666 Fifth Avenue
New York, New York 10103

This work was first published in Great Britain by Walker Books Ltd.

Designed by Wilma Robin

Library of Congress Cataloging in Publication Data
Daneman, Meredith.
    Francie and the boys / Meredith Daneman.
    p. cm.
    Summary: Despite her parents' objections, thirteen-year-old Francie becomes involved in a theatrical production at Dubbs' School for Boys, winning the lead role and the attention of two student actors.
    ISBN 0-440-50137-7
    [1. Theatre—Fiction. 2. England—Fiction.] I. Title.
PZ7.D213Fr 1989
[Fic]—dc19   88-13114
                                                                          CIP
                                                                          AC

Manufactured in the United States of America

February 1989

10 9 8 7 6 5 4 3 2 1

BG

To Flora

FRANCIE

═══ AND ═══

THE BOYS

1

"What about your schoolwork?" shouted Francie's father. "What about your *homework*? You have enough trouble keeping up as it is. I'm sorry, Frances, but it's out of the question."

"Wandsworth?" exclaimed her mother. "Did you say this boys' school was in Wandsworth? How are you planning to get back from there after dark? If you think I'm going to drive you backward and forward through that terrible one-way system, you've got another think coming."

"I'll get a bus," said Francie quietly. "I've got to do it. I've been chosen."

"Well," said her father sarcastically, "I'm sure it's a great honor. But there won't be much glory in failing your exams in the summer."

But her mother's tone had lightened. "How many did they choose?" she said.

"Six."

"Out of your class?"

"Out of the school."

Francie's parents looked at each other in surprise. It was not like Francie to get herself singled out.

"What do they want you for?" said her father. "I mean, what part do they want you to play?"

Francie took a deep breath. "I don't know," she said.

"You don't know?" they recited back in perfect unison. They were like a chorus in a play themselves.

"It's not written yet," said Francie carefully. "We're going to sort of make it up. As we go along."

"Improvisation!" cried her father triumphantly, as though he had just discovered a new dirty word. Francie's heart sank. Now he was really against it. Her parents never disapproved of things in a straightforward way like parents were supposed to. They had their own weird prejudices. Words like *improvisation* were like a red rag to a bull to her father. He was an illustrator of great craft and skill: he hated anything makeshift. As an artist, he liked things to be scientific. Making it up as you went along sounded to him like finger painting.

"They've got a *theme*," she said desperately. "Some incident that happened on Putney Heath in Victorian times. The history master's researching it. And the music master's already written the songs." She racked her brains for some way to include the math master as well in this academic lineup and looked appealingly at her mother, but she was still obsessed with geography. She'd got out a bus map and was busy establishing that there was no direct bus service between Wandsworth and Barnes. Francie couldn't think why she was bothering. When it came to it, her mother would be bound to insist on picking her up in the car. With all the open common land around Barnes, she worried a lot about the physical safety of her two daughters. That was why, against all her political beliefs, she'd sent them both to the local private girls' school just round the corner: not to get a better education, but because it was close.

"This school in Wandsworth is a comprehensive, you know," said Francie, playing now quite shamelessly on her mother's sense of guilt. "You're the one who's always going on about wanting me to mix with boys."

Boys, actually, were the last things Francie wanted to mix with. Excited as she was by the idea of the play, she dreaded the idea of acting with a bunch of pimply loudmouths. Then a flash came into her mind of a recent production at her own school of *Julius Caesar,* with bosomy sixth-formers wrapped in sheets striding manfully about the assembly hall, and determination rose in her once more. But her father had noticed the flaw in her argument.

"It can't be much of a comprehensive," he said sourly, "if it's a school for boys only."

"If they had girls there," said Francie impatiently, "they wouldn't want *me!*" Her voice was becoming unusually loud and piercing. "You've got to let me do it," she said, near tears. "It's not fair to stop me!"

Just then her sister, Jessica, burst into the room. "She's right, it's not fair!" she joined in, in sisterly solidarity, even though she didn't have a clue what they were arguing about, and then proceeded to attack her parents on some pretext of her own. Jessica had black hair and flashing eyes. People were always asking if she wanted to be an actress, but she didn't, she wanted to be a doctor. She was seventeen and about to embark on a dangerous mixture of A level exams and first love. No wonder Francie's mother and father forgot all about their younger daughter and switched their anxiety instantly to Jessica's latest crisis. Francie didn't mind in the least. She adored her sister and was delighted to hand over her parents in this mood. She left the three of them shouting at one another and went and sat on the stairs with the dog.

The dog was called Bat after the Battersea Dogs' Home and was thirteen, exactly the same age as Francie. Young enough for a person, it was a pretty decrepit age in a dog. But Francie felt maternal toward him. She could boss him around when other people bossed her, and comfort him when she felt like crying. Despite his woeful breath he had a saintly nature and was prepared to put up with anything from Francie for the honor of being her friend.

Francie was both cross and upset. It had been an exhausting enough day without this. Being chosen for the play when almost all her friends had been rejected had been extremely hard to handle. She'd had to go around all afternoon shrugging and pretending it was all terribly unimportant, that she wasn't particularly pleased. And then no sooner had she walked in the door, bursting to give vent to her excitement and pleasure at last, than there'd been this new opposition to contend with. What if her parents really wouldn't give in? How would she face her friends tomorrow? There was something so shaming about not being allowed to do things. People were always whispering in corners: "Miranda Fogarty isn't allowed to go to the fair," or "Harriet Parsons isn't allowed to watch *Dynasty.*" Her friends were a pretty broad-minded lot. To have an alcoholic mother or a jailbird father was definitely glamorous. The only real disgrace was to be forbidden.

But it wasn't just a matter of appearances. She herself was frankly amazed at how much she wanted to be in this play. She'd never been particularly interested in acting. When a scene from a Shakespeare play was read out in class, she was hardly ever given a part as she was always in a dream when it came to her cue, or had lost the place. She'd been in one of her famous dreams a week ago when it had been announced in assembly that the Sir Henry

Dubbs' School for Boys was to put on a musical at Easter and needed to recruit some girls to augment the cast. The preliminary auditions were to be held that day during the lunch hour. Anyone interested was to present herself in the assembly hall at one o'clock.

Francie had looked blank when her friends discussed their chances animatedly over their sandwiches, and would certainly not have gone along had they not taken her by the arm and yanked her there.

"Come *on*," they begged, as though it would give them confidence to have her with them. After all, someone as quiet and vague as Francie was hardly likely to be any competition.

2

Any idea Francie had of what auditions were like had been picked up watching old American movies on television starring Mickey Rooney. She'd expected to have to join a line of hopefuls trooping one by one onto the stage to deliver their quavering rendition of "Friends, Romans, countrymen," without the benefit of a white sheet, while from the back of the hall a voice in the dark called out, "Next, please."

What's more she was sure her sister would be there. This kind of thing was Jessica's territory and Francie didn't like to intrude on it, or set herself up to be judged a pale shadow of her dramatic sister.

But there was no sign of Jessica, although by the time Francie and her friends arrived the hall was quite crowded. No one was up on the stage; in fact most people had their backs to it and were gathered around a boyish-looking man in a baggy tracksuit with whom they seemed to be playing a clapping game. Another much bigger man with a beard sat to the side of the room at the piano, but he wasn't playing, his arms were folded because the clapping exercise wasn't something that could be done to music. It was anything but rhythmic: the idea was that you had to stretch your arms out stiffly in front of you and bring your hands together at exactly the same instant as the man in the middle—not a split second earlier or later —as though the hundred or so people in the room were one. The man laughed as he did it, trying to catch them out. It all looked pretty babyish to Francie, but even the sixth-formers were having a go, so she joined in and in fact found that it was more difficult than it appeared: it took a surprising amount of concentration to judge exactly when the leader would make his move. After a while there was quite a sense of achievement as even the dullest person in the room began to get the hang of it and the intermittent claps rang out, clear and rather thrillingly loud, like pistol shots.

The clapping man introduced himself to latecomers as Toby Lloyd (they could call him Toby) and his bearded colleague at the piano as Roy (call him Roy) Jackson. Francie had never had a male teacher, let alone one you were supposed to address by his Christian name, and she made up her mind to speak as little as possible. Toby seemed prepared to do all the talking anyway. He explained to them that what they had just been doing was an exercise in ensemble playing: what he and Roy were looking for was not necessarily people who liked getting up in front of everyone else and showing off, but people who could pull together and were alert and responsive to what was going on around them. There would be no star parts, he assured them, in the play they were putting on, but everyone in it would have an enormous contribution to make. It was going to be hard work, a lot of sweat; acting could sometimes be a painful process of self-exposure.

There were stifled giggles at the word *exposure*. Toby brushed impatiently at his forehead. He had a lock of hair at the front that fell constantly in his eyes.

"You'll hear worse things than that before this play gets on the stage," he said with a scowl. "Anyone likely to faint at a few four-letter words had better opt out right now." It was like a dare. He looked expectantly around the room. Of course, nobody left. A few people who had been put off by the lack of star parts and were thinking of excusing themselves, changed their minds and decided to stay after all. But Toby handed them over to Roy at this point, as though somehow they had lost his confidence with their prissiness.

Where Toby was thin and wiry, Roy was large and shambling. His belly hung out over his trousers when he stood up, and with his black beard and his rumbling fee-fi-fo-fum voice he reminded Francie of a giant. But he was not at all fearsome: instinctively she felt much less nervous of him than she did of Toby.

Roy went on to tell them a bit about the play, that there were to be local scenes in it: a dramatic duel on Putney Heath and a hilarious scene in Wandsworth police station; that it had a title, *An Affair of Honor*, which was actually ironic because it was about some most dishonorable goings-on. And although it was to be set in the 1840s, it would have a lot to say about the injustices and class divisions of today.

There was a bit of muttering at the back at this, as some of the more political sixth-formers began to suspect a left-wing tract. Toby stepped in swiftly and divided those present into two groups, the fifth- and sixth-formers to go with him to the gym, and Francie's lot, the third- and fourth-formers, to stay in the hall with Roy.

Roy sat them down on the floor and asked them to think back over their lives to some incident that had upset or frightened them. He asked for volunteers and there seemed no end to the stream of girls prepared to get up and confide their innermost fears to the world at large. There were hair-raising experiences with spiders, blood-curdling visits to the dentist, and spine-chilling encounters in haunted houses with ghosts. Francie was not particularly afraid of insects, had never had to have a tooth filled, and did not believe in ghosts. She felt dull and uninspired. Clearly, in order to be an actress it was necessary to have led a more dramatic life than she had. Roy had got past the volunteers now and was picking people at random. A girl was on her feet telling how she had saved her little brother from drowning. Francie could think of nothing so heroic to relate. Also she had the sneaky feeling that the girl was making it up. A friend of hers, Amanda, was next. She gave a rather vivid account of nearly being thrown from a horse as it bolted across a field. There was something oddly formal, not to say familiar, about the language Amanda was using and it struck Francie that she was quoting verbatim from an English essay she'd written that term entitled "A Visit to the Countryside," for which she'd received an illustrious A plus. Francie hoped and prayed she wouldn't be asked next, since the only thing she could think of describing—a scary ride on the big wheel at Barnes Common Fair—would seem tame and pathetic after such a literary brush with raw nature. But suddenly Roy's eyes, strangely pale-colored in his black-bearded face, lighted on her ducked head.

"You," he said. "Yes, you, with the pigtail."

Francie stood up, but as she did her wits seemed to fall right out of her head. She couldn't remember a word of what she'd planned to say. She looked around at the sea of expectant faces, all individually familiar to her, but merging now to form a new mass personality that she didn't take to at all.

And then, as though the very pressure of her panic was actually pressing a button in her mind, a strange thing happened. Something from the past rose up vividly in her memory, demanding to be recounted; a completely different story from the one she had planned to tell. She found herself describing something that had happened to her as a very little girl, telling them about it as it occurred to her, there and then.

She and her family were on the beach in Cornwall or somewhere, she couldn't for the moment remember. It was a hot, sticky afternoon and her parents went home to make some tea. Because the cottage where they were staying was so close, she and her big sister were allowed to stay and play on the sand by themselves. After a while she got tired of not being allowed to go in the water and wanted to go home, but Jessica was cross and would not come. So while her sister was busy poking a stick at some crabs in a rock pool, Francie wandered off by herself.

She knew the track from the beach to the row of little white matching cottages perfectly well. She had been backward and forward along it twice, sometimes four times, a day. The gate was open and so was the veranda door. As she walked in, there was a slightly strange disinfectant smell. Because of the bright sunlight it seemed very dark inside: she couldn't see at first. And then she heard barking, which was strange, as Bat had been left in London. Only it wasn't a dog barking, it was a human, with a cough so terrible it sounded like an animal. In the corner of the room sat an old man wrapped in a blanket, bending over a tin basin on his lap. Leaning over him so that Francie couldn't see her face was a woman wearing nothing but a petticoat and slippers. Her hair hung girlishly down over her shoulders, but it was white, brittle, *old* hair, and her skin sagged and had a bluish, bruised look. The air was heavy with dust and there was a sour smell that the disinfectant couldn't hide. Francie cleared her throat, and they raised their heads at the same moment, like twins. With their eyes bulging in their waxy faces they looked suddenly infantile in the creepy way that newborn babies look old. With an awful retching cough the old man tried to rise to his feet. The basin clattered to the floor. "Get out of here," the old woman gasped, and Francie ran, screaming. She ran out of the cottage, which was identical, of course, to the one next door where she was actually staying, screaming in terror. And what had made her scream like that wasn't the fact that the poor old couple were *not* her parents, but that for a moment she had thought that they *were*. In that room for that moment she had been convinced that the old man and woman must truly be her father and mother, changed out of all recognition, old and ill and pitiful, shouting at her to go away.

Francie sat down with a bump. The effect of her own story upon her had left her rather white-faced and shaky. She hadn't been very articulate, she knew. Her voice had been halting and low, and she'd had to stop several times to remember exactly how it had been, the heat of that day, the smell of that room. It was rather a revolting story, without one good joke in it, and she wished she hadn't told it. If only she could have been witty and lighthearted and made her friends laugh. She should have stuck to the fair on Barnes Common.

But Roy was smiling at her and asking her name.

"Frances Emmerson," someone else answered for her, before she had time to speak for herself. Amanda nudged her in the ribs.

"He wrote your name down," she whispered. "Did you notice if he wrote down mine?"

3

Over the next few days there had been much speculation as to who would be chosen. Apparently a short-list was to go up on the bulletin board the following Monday and the successful girls would be called back for a final audition.

"I was rubbish, you were brilliant," everyone had gone around saying, hoping to be contradicted. But by the end of the week other events had taken precedence—an impending hockey match, a math test—and Francie, much taken up with her loathing for both math and hockey, had put the audition out of her mind to the extent that she hadn't even mentioned it at home.

She wished she had now. What her parents needed more than anything was time to get used to things. They would give in on most points, as long as they were properly prepared. If only Jessica would realize that.

The living room door slammed and her sister came tearing up the stairs in tears, pushing past Francie and Bat where they sat on the landing. Arguments between Jessica and her parents always ended in deadlock. For all her brilliance at science, Jessica was useless when it came to psychology. Francie's heart sank and Bat gave a great sympathetic sigh, as though he understood that now her mother and father would be in a worse mood than ever.

"God, Bat, you do stink," said Francie. She took him down to the kitchen to get him a bowl of water. While she was there she got some lime juice for herself and Jessica and carried both glasses to the top of the house. She dripped the lime a bit, going too fast up the stairs, and paused responsibly to rub the damp, sticky patch with the hem of her school tunic, which was a ghastly shade of bottle green anyway. But when she reached Jessica's attic room the door was locked and she couldn't make herself heard above the blare from Jessica's record player. Jessica's actual taste was for classical music, but when she was upset she played pop records at a deafening pitch.

Francie went back down to her own room, which was on the landing below. She closed the door, drank both drinks straight down, and put on some rival music of her own. A moment later the door was flung open and Jessica burst in. "Must you play that so loudly?" she said, and lifted the needle from Francie's record so that the music from her own room predominated once more. She didn't look a bit as though she'd been crying. Her eyelashes were stuck together not with damp tears but with freshly applied mascara.

"I brought you up a lime drink," said Francie, "but you didn't answer your door."

"Oh, darling, sorry," said Jessica.

"So I drank it."

"Selfish cow. Anyway I don't want lime, I want whisky."

They both knew she was lying since she'd often admitted to Francie that she hated the taste of spirits. The most she could manage was rum and Coke. "I'm going to meet some friends at the pub. Can I borrow your blue sweater?"

"No," said Francie. "It'll make you look even more underage than you are. What about cramming for your exams?"

"Stuff it," said Jessica. "It'll be Their fault if I fail all my exams." She pulled Francie's blue sweater out of her cupboard and held it up against her in front of the mirror. "Go on," she said. "I've got nothing to wear. I'm not prepared to borrow something of Mum's when she's been so horrible to me."

The color did suit her. Better than it suited Francie. "You'll stretch it," Francie said, but secretly she was flattered that Jessica wanted to borrow something of hers. You had to admit that Jessica was glamorous. She had had her dark hair permed and it frizzed out from her face in a wild and woolly cloud. She had a curly mouth and flaring nostrils and a deep furrow of fury in her forehead when she scowled. Next to hers, Francie's looks seemed hopelessly mild and grave.

"Oh, all right," said Francie. "But only for tonight. And you'll have to wash it if you're going to the pub. I don't want it back stinking of beer and smoke."

"Thanks," said Jessica and was out of what she was wearing and into the blue sweater in a flash, pushing it up at the sleeves, tugging it down at the hips, reorganizing the collar, until it looked like something that had always and only been hers.

"It's great," she said, with a radiant smile, made entirely happy by something new to wear, and was gone, back to her room, singing along with the music, leaving her discarded sweater inside out on Francie's floor.

Francie picked it up with a sigh, turned it the right way in, and followed her. Jessica's room was like a nest, lined with open books, screwed-up papers, and records out of their covers. Crossing her floor you had to leap for the small patches of blank carpet left uncovered. The desk, strangely, was quite neat, importantly set out with textbooks and pens. But Jessica was sitting at her chaotic dressing table, painting her lips with a brush.

Francie put the sweater in a drawer and picked her way over to the unmade bed. She cleared a space and sat down cautiously.

"You know the musical they were auditioning for at school," she began.

"Mmm?"

"The one Dubbs' Boys are putting on. They wanted girls for it."

"Oh, yes. I decided not to try for it. Because of my exams. I can't afford the time. Not that I suppose They'll give me any credit for that. They never do take into account the things I *do* give up."

"I got in."

Jessica swiveled in her seat and stared.

"What, into the play?"

Francie nodded.

"They chose you?" Jessica crossed the room, not caring where she trod, and hugged Francie. "Well done," she said. "That's really brilliant, Francie."

Francie rubbed her cheek where Jessica's painted lips had left an imprint. "I'm a bit amazed," she said. "I thought I was useless at the auditions. I still think they must have made a mistake."

"Nonsense," said Jessica. "I've always thought you were a brilliant mimic. You can do any accent. And you *are* my sister."

They both laughed.

"The only trouble is," said Francie seriously, "They won't let me do it. Daddy says I can't because of my work, and Mummy says it's too far away."

"Same old crap they're still giving me," said Jessica. "Don't worry, *I'll* talk to them."

"No," said Francie hastily. "I expect I can handle it." She was suddenly relieved that Jessica was going out. When it came to diplomacy, her sister was a liability. But it was nice to have someone on her side. "I think I'll go and have a bath now and get into my pajamas before dinner. That'll give me time to do the washing-up for them afterward."

"You are a canny one," said Jessica, laughing. "All right, then, play it your own way. Only I think there's a principle at stake here. By the way, don't tell Them I've gone to the pub, will you. Say I've gone to Sadie's."

Downstairs in the bathroom Francie locked the door. She'd taken to doing that lately. Her father could be relied on to knock, but the female members of the family had a tendency to burst in unannounced. Her breasts were only just beginning, and her pubic hair was quite fair and sparse, but if they walked in when she was undressing, or in the bath, they didn't seem to be able to stop their eyes from wandering to her body or, worse still, to refrain from making dreadful patronizing personal remarks about how nicely she was coming along. Her mother was the worst offender at this sort of thing. She was always talking openly to Francie about sex to make up for the fact that *her* mother had been so secretive. Personally, Francie thought that her grandmother had known when to shut up.

She poured a bit too much of her mother's bath oil into the water and lay soaking in the vaporous warmth. She loved washing nowadays. And yet such a short time ago it had seemed such a chore, she'd hardly had the patience to stay in the water long enough to soak her armpits. Now she had gone the other way: She was becoming a well-known bathroom hog. Her thoughts floated with her limbs and her worries seemed to rise above the water with the steam, leaving her to recall unclouded the earlier events of the day.

4

"Have you seen the bulletin board?" Amanda had said excitedly as Francie drifted into the classroom that morning.

Francie had looked blank.

"We're on the short-list. For the Dubbs' play, twit face. You and me and Sarah, and Rosanna Hawthorn in the other lower fourth. No one else in our year. We've got to go to the gym at lunchtime."

Francie wondered for a moment if it might be April the first, but it wasn't, it was the fifteenth of October. The bell had rung for assembly, so it was too late to check on the bulletin board: she would have to take Amanda's word for it. Across the crowded assembly hall, Sarah, who wasn't a particular friend of hers, gave her a surprisingly intimate smile. Rosanna Hawthorn looked straight through her, but then Rosanna Hawthorn was in the other class and thought to be slightly deranged.

Usually, while the headmistress droned on, Francie ran

her eyes over the engraved lists of ancient head girls and scholarship winners, whose names she knew by heart. But today her mind raced ahead to the lunch hour and to what emotional contortions might be required of her among the wall bars and vaulting horses and rubber mats. She wondered if she should take a tip from Amanda and read up on some of her old compositions: "A Person I Admire," "My Favorite Pet," "A Winter's Day." But that might do more harm than good. She did not get A's for English like Amanda. And anyway, how could you practice to be spontaneous?

At break she discovered her name *was* on the short-list: F. Emmerson, second from the bottom. She ate her sandwiches then and there, afraid that she might have trouble getting them down in a hurry at lunchtime. Just as well, for when the lunch bell actually rang, she found she needed time to get to the lavatory. How did she seriously imagine she could take part in a play, when she couldn't even make it to the audition without her insides turning to water?

"Quick!" said Amanda, who was waiting for her outside the gym. Hardly any of the upper sixths had come back, Francie noticed: like Jessica they were too busy with exams to dare to get involved. Roy, who was marking off names on a list, looked up as they entered and smiled. "It's Amanda, isn't it, and Frances?" he said, and Francie was flattered and impressed to have her name got right even if he *had* only worked it out by a process of elimination.

"Right," said Toby, the knees of his tracksuit baggier than ever. He appeared not to have changed his clothes or combed his unruly hair since their last encounter. "I'm going to divide you off into pairs and give you a little scenario to act out for me. Let it develop any way you like —the situation I describe need only be a starting point." Francie stuck close to Amanda for moral support, but

Toby wanted them to break new ground. Amanda was paired off with a buxom fifth-former, and Francie was obliged to take up with mad Rosanna.

She would have liked to have seen how the other couples went about it, but they weren't encouraged to watch. They were advised to go outside onto the staff lawn and discuss the scene with their partner until they were called. As a rule, the staff lawn was out of bounds to pupils, and officious prefects kept marching up to the rehearsing couples and ordering them off the grass.

"We're *allowed!*" the pairs would chorus grandly, and then put their heads back together again, plotting their important strategies.

All except Francie and Rosanna. Francie found her partner's attention impossible to engage.

"Christ, what a bore," Rosanna said, and lay down flat on her back on one of the garden seats, with her eyes closed. Francie hardly liked to disturb her. She was a remote, haughty-looking girl with a rather distinguished profile. Francie considered leaving her there and going back to the lavatory and locking herself in with the lunchtime smokers until the whole embarrassing ordeal was over. Let Rosanna play the scene with herself. She could be both husband and wife as far as Francie was concerned. In the scenario they'd been given, the husband's boss was supposed to have made a pass at the wife. The husband was angry and the wife was supposed to try to calm him down. Any moment now they would be called back to the gym and they hadn't even discussed who was to be who, let alone what on earth they were going to say to each other.

Suddenly Rosanna opened her eyes. "With my haircut I'd better be the husband," she said. "Not that it'll make any difference. I don't suppose they've come all the way to a girls' school to choose someone who looks like a boy."

"What rubbish, you don't," said Francie, and meant it. For all her brutally shorn head Rosanna's features were delicate and her expression unusually vulnerable. Suddenly Francie felt sorry for her. It was rumored that her parents had recently split up and not for the usual commonplace reason of her father going off with another woman. Apparently Rosanna's father had gone off with another man. Even in the worldly atmosphere of the lower fourth, this had caused a slight stir.

"I'll play the husband if you like," said Francie. "I don't care which way around it is as long as we sort it out."

"No," said Rosanna fiercely, sitting up. "I can't play the wife. I despise her. 'Calm him down!' How pathetic. I'd rather be the man."

Francie shrugged. Now was not the moment to try to deal with Rosanna's identity problems. "Okay," she said. "I'll play the wife. How shall we start?"

"Oh, just say whatever comes into our heads," said Rosanna. "That's supposed to be the point of this ridiculous exercise, isn't it?"

In one way, Rosanna was the perfect partner. What came into her head when the moment arrived was so outlandish and took up so much of Francie's attention that she simply didn't have time to be nervous. In another way the girl was a nightmare. She started shouting at Francie the moment they entered the gym, treating Toby and Roy, who sat side by side on the vaulting horse with their arms folded, as though they didn't exist.

"You might as well tell me what happened," Rosanna shouted. "I'm bound to find out in the end. Just exactly what did this man do to you? Where did he touch you? Exactly how and where?"

Francie stared at Rosanna in real hatred. How could she do this to her? "I don't think we need to go into details," she said quietly. "It wasn't very serious. He didn't do me any harm."

"Harm?" shrieked Rosanna. "How can you tell how much harm's been done? He's harmed me for a start." She sat down on one of the rubber mats and started sobbing in a most unmanly way. "It's disgusting," she hiccuped, "How could you let him do it?"

Francie was horrified. It was clear that Rosanna was acting out some ghastly domestic trauma of her own. It was now Francie's genuine, overwhelming desire to "calm her down" before she gave away any more embarrassing secrets of her home life. She sat down beside her and put her arm around her shoulders.

"Thomas," she said, christening her on the spot in an attempt to draw her out of reality and back into the story. "Don't worry about it so much. Nobody minds about that sort of thing these days. Come on, Thomas, get up and I'll make you some tea. I've got some really jammy doughnuts I bought on the way home from school, I mean the office."

"I'm not hungry," said Rosanna sulkily, but she got up, curiously obedient to her new name, and crossed to the wall bars. She stood with her back to Francie, hanging on to the rungs above her head.

Roy nudged Toby and muttered something.

"Thomas," said Francie desperately, "can't you say something?"

Suddenly Rosanna swung around, laughing eerily. She was certainly giving them the full benefit of her emotional range. "I'll kill him," she said, her almond-shaped eyes gleaming in a shaft of sunlight. "That's what I'll do. I'll get a gun and kill him."

"I think that might be going a bit far," said Francie drily. All this melodrama was not really to her taste. She tried to break up the atmosphere with a little joke. "Anyway, you can't kill your boss, you'll get the sack." She giggled hopefully and to her relief Roy and Toby joined in.

"It's me you're all laughing at," said Rosanna, tears flooding back into her eyes, and Francie had had enough. She dropped her silly wife guise and said with her own true brand of sympathy: "It's not, Rosanna, honestly it isn't."

She looked for help to Toby and Roy, but they were as absorbed and cheerful as if they were watching television. Glued to the sight of Rosanna's raw emotional state, they seemed prepared for her to go on indefinitely in this precarious vein. It was then that it first struck Francie that in the cause of art they might not be entirely kind. "I think we ought to stop now," she said with unexpected authority. "If you don't mind."

"Right. Yes. Fine," said Toby. He turned to Roy and they exchanged a muttered word. "I think perhaps we'd like to hear you sing," he said.

Both girls turned away, automatically thinking he meant the other. "I mean both of you," said Toby impatiently. "We'd like you both to come back when we've seen the rest. Come to the assembly hall at about ten to two."

"What do you want us to sing?" said Rosanna, in a perfectly normal voice. Francie stared at her. Had all that hysterical behavior been just acting after all?

"Anything you like," said Toby. "As long as it's fairly well known. Roy can play most things if he's heard the tune."

"Just a verse of something will do," added Roy. "A nursery rhyme if necessary. We don't need a great aria."

Francie wasn't fussy what she sang as long as it wasn't a duet with Rosanna. Their domestic intimacy over, the two girls went back out into the playground, strangers again.

Amanda and Sarah, who'd been in earlier, were waiting for Francie to see how she'd got on.

"It was pretty embarrassing," said Francie. "How was yours?"

"Not bad," said Amanda. "Sarah's went really well. Poor you, though, being stuck with Rosanna."

"Actually," said Francie, "Rosanna was rather good. They really seemed to like her. I think she'll get in, if she can sing."

"Sing?" said Sarah and Amanda in unison, and Francie realized at once that neither of them had been asked back. They had not got in. She blushed for them, a stinging, burning blush that started deep inside her, to think that they had been left like this, not knowing.

"You've got to sing, too, haven't you?" said Amanda. Her face was a bit twisted, but she was smiling. She was a good friend. "Well done, Francie. You must have done really well."

"I'm not in yet," said Francie. "I've still got to sing. There are miles better people than me."

"I don't care anyway," said Sarah. "I'd never have been able to fit it in with my ballet. It was really stupid making us make it up like that. Why couldn't they have given us proper lines to say?"

"Yes," said Francie, "I don't see how they can judge from what we did. They must just be looking for certain types."

"Such as Rosanna," said Amanda, unable to curb the bitchiness in her voice.

"Rosanna is weird," said Francie. "But I think she's a natural actress. Whatever that is." It was strange, the loyalty she could feel for Rosanna, without liking her. It was as though they had faced some danger together which had made them comrades whether they wanted to be or not. But she didn't want to upset Amanda further. "What shall I sing?" she said helplessly. "I haven't got the faintest idea what to choose," and that brought out the best in both girls. Suddenly they saw Francie as their best hope, batting on alone for the glory of their class. They set about coaching her for the next round.

"What about that one we did for Miss Reynolds," said Sarah eagerly. "You know, 'Jesu Joy of Man's Thingummybob.'"

"It's not a church choir she's trying for," said Amanda. "Something from a musical would be better."

Although Francie was in the junior choir, she wasn't considered much of a singer. Her poor sight-reading hadn't endeared her to the music mistress, and as her voice was rather low and husky, she always sang the second or third part: the solos always went to the showy sopranos. But she had a pleasant, tuneful tone, and Amanda and Sarah were pleased with their pupil. They wanted her at first to sing "Doe-a-Deer," but when Francie protested she hated *The Sound of Music,* they settled on "Wouldn't It Be Luverly?" from *My Fair Lady.*

"Make sure you start in F," said Sarah.

"Don't forget the cockney accent," said Amanda. "And sing up."

This last lap of the audition was the bit that worried Francie least. The dashing of Amanda's hopes had made success seem unimportant: it would be more friendly to fail. Time was running out for Roy and Toby. The bell for afternoon lessons had already gone and they had to make a decision. They had to listen to twelve people sing and choose six, and there was really only one way to do it—by knock-out competition. They were reduced in the end to the kind of auditioning technique that Francie had first expected. True, you didn't actually have to go up on the stage to sing; you were allowed to stand close to the piano, which was at the side of the hall, so that Roy could watch at the same time as he accompanied. But you did have to line up without ceremony and do your bit with everybody staring, and some people were rather rudely stopped and thanked before they were even halfway through their song. And to her surprise Francie found that there was a kind of rough justice in this simple, straightforward method. You could tell almost as soon as people opened their mouths whether or not they would do. It was obvious who would be chosen. They *must,* for instance, pick Isabel Archer, a friend of Jessica's and the only sixth-former left in the running. Seniority apart, she had a lovely trained-sounding voice and had distinguished herself in the school play as Mark Antony to Jessica's Brutus. Rosanna would definitely get in, despite singing "Pop Goes the Weasel" in an unexpectedly quavering voice. And when, quite calmly and objectively, she heard her own voice ringing out, without vibrato and quite surprisingly loud in the echoing acoustic, she never once doubted that Toby and Roy would let her sing all four verses through without interruption. "Oh, wo—o—o—dn't it be luverlee!" she sang, fired by the joy of having already missed ten minutes of math. When she was finished, Roy smiled and nodded to her from the piano with what seemed to her to be shameless favoritism.

"Right," said Toby, when the flat and tone-deaf among them had been dismissed. "You're our six girls. We'll be sending you a rehearsal schedule and a form for your parents to sign in due course. Any questions?"

Of course there were none. No one dared say, well, now that I've been chosen, can I think about this? Exactly what am I taking on? What part will I get to play, what am I committing myself to—is this wise? Everyone including Francie just stood there smiling sheepishly, stupid with relief, as though the whole thing were over, instead of just beginning.

5

"Have you gone to sleep in there?" shouted Francie's mother, banging on the bathroom door. "I've been calling and calling you to dinner. Have you drowned, or what?"

"Just coming," called Francie jumping out of the bathwater which had turned cold and was quite unclouded by any hint of soap. She would have to rely on the bath oil to make her smell nice.

"What's that awful smell you've put on yourself, Frances?" said her father as she rushed into the dining room in her blue striped pajamas. "You smell like a tart's armpit."

Her father had a graphic turn of phrase that was usually a source of great delight to Francie. On any ordinary evening she would have pointed out that it was he who had chosen the scent himself, for his wife. As the youngest member of the family, she had a license for cheekiness and could get away with nicking her mother's best beauty potions. But tonight there was too much at stake. She had already stretched her luck by being late. Her mother and father had started eating, and Jessica's empty place drew attention to itself, spoiling the atmosphere like an unpleasant guest. She said nothing and sat down meekly in front of her shepherd's pie.

"She might have warned me if she didn't want any dinner," said her mother, speaking, as nearly always these days, of Jessica. "Did she tell you where she was going, Francie?"

"She said something about going to Sadie's," said Francie quickly, and shoveled a large forkful of pie into her mouth before she could be expected to answer any more questions. Francie was a dreadful fusspot over food and shepherd's pie was not a thing she cared for. She like all the things that were in it individually—the meat, the carrots, the tomatoes, the potatoes. It was the mixing up of all these tastes that put her off. That, and her father's stupid jokes about bits of old shepherd floating around in gravy. But for once she refrained from pulling faces.

"This is delicious," she said instead, to ingratiate herself with her mother. She munched avidly and licked her lips and made little murmuring noises of delight with every mouthful. And to her surprise she was fooled by her own performance. In pretending to enjoy it she found that she actually did. Apparently, to an actress of conviction, even shepherd's pie could be quite tasty. This new proof of her talent prompted her to speak.

"Did you think any more about the Dubbs' Boys play?" she said softly.

Too softly. Her mother was still communing with the empty chair.

"Perhaps I'd better put some back in the oven," she was saying, "in case she comes in, in a minute, starving hungry."

"Don't do any such thing," said Francie's father. "How

dare she go out without saying what time she'd be back. This isn't a hotel."

"She probably doesn't realize how late it is. Her watch is broken."

"It would be. Fine doctor she'll make if she can't keep her wristwatch alive."

"It's not the time that worries me, it's the dark. I don't like her out on her own near the common. I bought her a rape alarm, but she's let the batteries go flat."

Francie sighed. Sometimes you could hardly blame Jessica for not coming home. Yet she felt sorry for her parents as well. It was hard for them, having to be cross and worried all the time, to be thought of as Them. Particularly when they prided themselves on their liberal attitudes. Her father, although pompous, could be really funny and often said outrageous things like "tart's armpit," which scandalized her friends more than the far filthier swear words they used themselves at school. Her mother was hopelessly vague and didn't concentrate. She illustrated children's books and spent a lot of time with her eyes half closed converting the world into shapes and colors. But she was less determinedly grown up than most of the other mothers Francie knew. You'd never believe that some of them had once been flower children in love with Mick Jagger. Francie's mother had long hair and swapped clothes with Jessica. But all this worrying was beginning to spoil her face. And Francie's dad, who used to be so much fun, was getting more and more bad-tempered over studying and exams. It was as though Jessica, just by being seventeen, had turned them into typical parents. And now she herself, at thirteen, was threatening to start the same trick.

But she would not give up the play. There was something cold and stony about the way she felt when she thought about it. Her father's cross voice and her mother's anxious face would not move her. She would hold out till she won. And because they loved her they would have to give in. She suddenly saw that the important thing to do was to make giving in easy for them.

"You know, you'd really approve of the two men who are directing this play," she said.

"What play, dear?" said her mother vaguely.

"The one I was telling you about," said Francie patiently. "The one I've been asked to be in. You'd really like them. They're really modern and outspoken. Some of the girls giggled at the words they used and they told them not to be so prissy. If I'm not allowed to be in it, it might look as though you're too prissy to let me."

Her parents looked at each other in amusement. She knew they were laughing at her attempt at diplomacy, but she didn't care as long as they were good-humored.

"Goodness," said her father, "we can't have that."

"And," said Francie, "I think the story might be going to be a bit on the left-wing side." With an enormous effort of memory she managed to quote what Roy had said. "Even though it's set in the 1840s, it's going to have a lot to say about the injustices and class divisions of today."

She took a deep breath, but her parents had stopped smiling. They were looking at her with something bordering on respect.

"*And*," said Francie, getting excited, "there aren't going to be any starring parts. Everybody has to pull together, like a team."

"What?" said her father incredulously, and Francie knew she had gone too far. "This is a play you're talking about, Frances, not a football match. Don't give me all that guff about everybody being equal. Come to me when it's over and tell me there were no starring parts."

Despite his socialist ideals, it seemed to Francie that when it came to the arts her father was a bit of a fascist.

But something he had said had lifted her heart. What was it? "Come to me when it's over . . ."

"I'm sure I'll find out you're right," she said, shamelessly compliant when it came to advancing her cause. "I'm sure when I've had personal experience I'll agree with you."

But her father was off on one of his diatribes. *He* had had personal experience: he'd done a bit of designing for the theater in his early days, enough to make him realize what a ruthless, competitive business it was. It was no place for a grown professional person to try to make a living. Francie, who only wanted to be in a school play, looked around helplessly to her mother, but she had taken the opportunity to slip out to the kitchen with the remains of the shepherd's pie, to keep it hot in the oven for Jessica.

Francie was on the verge of tears. "Look, Dad," she said when he was finished, "I haven't made up my mind to be an actress or anything. And if it's so awful, wouldn't it be better if I found out now?"

Her mother had come back in with a bowl of fruit. She sat down and started peeling an orange. She broke up the segments and passed them to Francie's father. Peeling fruit for her husband was something she did when she was going to have her way.

"I've been thinking about it," she said, "and I think I could probably manage the journeys, at least at first. After a while we might find someone else in the cast who lives in Barnes who Francie could travel back with on the bus."

"We'll have to see how her schoolwork goes," said her father doubtfully. "If it shows any sign of suffering—"

The front door banged. Jessica was home. Francie saw her parents' faces harden as they braced themselves for the battle ahead. But her own battle had been won. They had said yes. Well, sort of yes. Yes in the only way parents can ever manage: by stopping saying no. She was going to be in the play.

Now for the very first time, she allowed herself to contemplate what that might mean. And instead of the cloudless summit of happiness she was expecting to imagine, she suddenly found herself picturing a very slippery slope indeed, peopled not just by a tyrant in a tracksuit and a bearded giant, but by those weird, wild alien beings commonly known as boys.

6

Even at four-thirty in the afternoon, after school hours, Dubbs Boys' School was teeming with activity. Francie, who was used to the genteel Edwardian-house atmosphere of her own school, felt as though she had arrived at an air terminal rather than an institute of learning. Decaying "contemporary" buildings surrounded a concrete courtyard. Dubbs had been built at a time of hope and optimism, and although it was down-at-heel now and in desperate need of a coat of paint, let alone more textbooks and more teachers, the sheer size and scale of the place left Francie's school for dead. They had everything here: a real theater, even a swimming pool. The only things they seemed to be short on were lavatories. The girls could not find anywhere to go.

Of course, there was the boys' cloakroom, a huge concrete edifice in the courtyard, but heaven knew what might meet your eye if you put your head around the door to *that* hellhole. Apparently there was no privacy in there at all, just rows of doorless cubicles with a watery steel wall for peeing up against, which of course was anatomically impossible if you happened to be a girl. If you could bring yourself to walk past these, and worse, past the communal showers beyond, there *were* some proper lavatories with doors, but the locks were broken and there was no paper, not even the hard sort that everybody complained about at Francie's school. Rosanna, who was the only one who dared go in there when it was empty, while the other girls stood guard outside, came out reeling from the smell and the things she had seen written on the walls. There were puddles everywhere, she said, and not all of them were rainwater.

The girls got extremely militant about the situation, and Francie fully expected Isabel Archer as the eldest of the group to lodge a formal complaint to Toby and Roy. But the odd thing was, as soon as they got inside the rehearsal room where the cast was gathered, the girls seemed to forget all about the fullness of their bladders and the persecution of their gender, and changed into cool, carefree creatures, constituted like camels.

The rehearsal room was painted a dingy color, as though its walls had been stained with nicotine. Any natural light had been blotted out by black curtains drawn across the windows. A complicated system of spotlights shone like searchlights from the high vaulted ceiling. The girls stood in the shadows at one end of the room and the boys crowded together in the center. Neither group took the slightest notice of the other. This was a more difficult feat for the girls, as they were outnumbered, five to one. The day was to dawn when Francie would come to appreciate such a ratio. But today she could only see it as a disadvantage. Like the lavatories, it seemed to her to be plain unfair.

Although they made no attempt to be friendly, Francie

couldn't help thinking that the boys were adjusting their behavior to attract attention. They talked and laughed extra loudly and peppered their conversation with words to shock and impress. Unlike the girls, they didn't have to wear school uniform and had consequently invented their own way of looking exactly the same as each other in jeans and T-shirts, with bomber jackets hooked on the forefinger and slung over the shoulder. The girls, on the other hand, stuck with their dreary green tunics, had developed a genius for looking individual, with the shoulder padding of blazers, the ironing out of regulation pleats, and the rolling up and down of shirt sleeves and ankle socks. Subtle shades of green had been achieved by dropping a cupful of bleach in the weekly wash. The only optional item, the green-and-white-striped tie, was worn optionally, anywhere but at the neck: as a low-slung belt, a knee bandage, or as a ribbon to tie back the hair.

There was no sign of Roy, but suddenly Toby emerged from the center of the crowd, where he had been posing as one of the boys.

"Right," he said, taking the floor. He gathered the girls into the group and made everyone sit down.

"Here we all are. Some of you are complete strangers to one another. Relish the moment. It won't last long. In a very short space of time we'll know each other all too well. Acting is a pretty revealing business. But today, let's use our ignorance to play a game. Let's see what we're like at snap character-judgments."

The game was this: A boy was to stand up and the girls were to call out one word that they thought, from his appearance, might best describe his character. Francie was irritated. This embarrassing exercise seemed to her to be typical of Toby. She wanted him to put himself forward for judgment so that she could call out, "Tease! Bully! Baggypants!" She looked around at the other girls for support, but they were all in thrall to Toby, who in the company of all these spotty youths seemed unexpectedly handsome and debonair.

A stocky boy called Simon with a rather red face got to his feet.

"Shy," suggested one girl, shyly. "Nervous," offered another.

The boys roared with laughter. Simon was obviously quite the reverse.

"You're giving me emotions you're feeling yourselves," said Toby. "Look again."

The girls stared. The unfortunate Simon grew redder. If he had never been shy or nervous in his life, he certainly was now.

"Reliable," said Isabel Archer, to let him off the hook.

"That's better," said Toby. "Now it's your turn."

Isabel looked sorry she'd spoken, but she got gamely to her feet. At the sight of her fair hair and curvy figure there were wolf whistles from the boys' camp and someone shouted, "Sexy!" Isabel kept her head. Her beautiful cream-colored skin did not color. She gazed levelly at the boys, who grew quiet and respectful.

"Cool," said one boy, to whom there was obviously no higher praise. And her reputation began to grow by the second: "Intelligent!" "Mature!" "Self-possessed."

Isabel, who could so easily withstand their rudeness, was completely thrown by their gallantry. She covered her face with her hands and sat down hurriedly.

"Richard," said Toby to the boy who had come up with "self-possessed," "let's have you next."

A much older, taller boy got languidly to his feet. He had sandy hair and spiky eyelashes that were paler than his eyes. He turned his head slightly sideways and his cold, insolent gaze seemed to be directed straight at Francie. To her surprise she felt for the first time prompted to speak. She did not say exactly the word that came to her, which was "conceited." "Proud!" she called out instead, before she could stop herself.

The boy raised his eyebrows and the corners of his fleshy mouth flicked in amusement. Francie felt sure he would wait for some more flattering assessment, but perhaps to punish her, he gave a mock bow of concession and sat down, as though handing the floor to her.

"All right, Frances," said Toby. "On your feet."

Francie got up. She took a deep breath and tried to outgaze the boys as Isabel had done, but what with the spotlight in her eyes, the best she could manage was a sort of swivel-eyed squint. There was a rather unflattering silence. Nobody seemed to be prepared to make anything of her at all. Rosanna nudged the boy sitting nearest to her and whispered something to him. "Dreamy," he repeated doubtfully. "Introspective," said another boy, taking up the clue, and "Quiet," said yet another.

Suddenly the conceited boy with the sandy hair spoke up, breaking the rules by using any number of words he liked. "She *looks* docile enough," he said loudly, "but it's my guess she's quite an assertive little thing. And rather skeptical about all this. A bit of a dissident, in fact."

Francie had never hated anyone so much in her life. He didn't even know her! How dare he presume to sum her up like that and in words she could barely understand. She understood one word well enough. *Little.* He had called her a "little thing." For that, alone, she was determined never to forgive him.

7

Francie sat down, her blood boiling. A curly-haired boy sitting near her reached over and put a hand on her arm.

"Don't worry," he said kindly, in a low voice. "No one really believes you're any of those things. Take no notice of Richard. He's an awful tease."

Toby noted the boy's sympathy and immediately picked on him to be the next public target. His name turned out to be Joe. To go with his dark tousled hair he had brown acne-free skin and clear blue eyes. The girls loved him on sight. "Kind!" they called out. "Strong!" "Honest!"

At this breathless point Roy came shambling into the room. Toby motioned to honest Joe to sit down, and the game died abruptly, as though it was the sort of fun that could be indulged in only when Roy's back was turned. Although he himself had been happy to stand, Toby fetched his colleague a chair, swinging it athletically over his head and placing it in the center of the group. Then he sat down on the bare boards like one of the boys, with his knees hugged up to his chest, a position his fat friend couldn't possibly have assumed.

Roy didn't mind being made to look overweight. In fact he liked to pretend he was even bigger than he was. He sat down heavily on the flimsy chair, stretching his legs out in front of him and leaning back to cause as many creaks as he could. Francie was relieved to see him. He had with him a sheaf of papers that she hoped might be something businesslike, such as a script, with lines of pre-arranged dialogue, or songs, actually written down. But he made no use of the pages except to fan his face and neck with them, as though to a large, hairy person such as himself, the room was unduly hot. Francie had taken him to be the musical director, but he seemed bent on giving them an out-of-hours history lesson.

"We've chosen the subject for this musical," he began, "because it's a bit of our own local past. You all know where the windmill is on Wimbledon Common. Well, just down the road from there is the spot where the parishes of Wimbledon, Putney, and Wandsworth meet. In the early nineteenth century, this used to be a dark, lonely place with no one around except the odd highwayman. A perfect spot for a duel. Lots of famous people came here for satisfaction. Lord Castlereagh, William Pitt, you name them, they all came to Putney. Samuel Pepys came, too, in 1667, but his idea of satisfaction wasn't fighting—he came to look at the girls. Anyone here heard of the Earl of Cardigan?"

He looked around expectantly. Were they, as actors, supposed to put their hands up?

"Come on!" he boomed. "Cardigan. What was he famous for?"

"Woolly sweaters," piped up a small boy facetiously.

"That's true, as it happens," said Roy. "The article of

clothing we know as a cardigan was in fact named after the earl."

The boy's face fell. In the circles he moved, the idea was to be funny, not right.

"Actually," said Roy, "speaking of knitting, it's the name of a woolly hat I'm looking for."

"Balaclava," said Isabel Archer, in the apologetic voice of a girl who hesitates to be a blue-stocking in the company of men.

And then conceited Richard spoke up for the boys, in a tired, drawling tone that managed to convey that he had known the answer all along.

"Half a league, half a league,
Half a league onward,
All in the valley of death
Rode the six hundred,"

he recited, as though it explained everything.

Trust him to speak in bloody poetry, thought Francie.

"Right," said Roy. "We know who we're talking about. The famous Lord Cardigan of the Charge of the Light Brigade. Except that that's *not* what our play's about."

Francie shot a triumphant look in Richard's direction. So he hadn't been so clever after all.

"Our subject is a much earlier incident in the same Lord Cardigan's life," said Roy. "It's all about a duel he fought on Putney Heath with an ex-captain of his regiment, Harvey Tuckett, and the farcical court case that followed."

Roy went on to explain the historical details, with much reference to marching soldiers, policemen in funny hats, and half-witted peers of the realm. It all sounded great fun for the boys, but where did the girls come in? Had they been through all that complicated selection process just for the chance of walking on? Roy had mentioned a couple of female parts, a miller's wife, a Mrs. Cunningham, but no one to compare with the heroic Tuckett or the villainous Cardigan. You could hardly blame a boys' school for favoring boys. But the girls had come all the way from Barnes. Was Isabel Archer expected to put her A levels at risk, merely to be part of the scenery?

But suddenly, as though he were a famous mind reader as well as a so-so pianist, Roy got up, knocking over his unfortunate chair, and crossed to the piano. He sat down and belted out a rather romantic number, to which he began to sing the words in a high falsetto voice of surprising beauty.

"He did it just for me," sang Roy,

"Though I never asked him to,
Though his life would never be the same,
He never spoke a word of blame,
He did it just for me."

If Francie had not been sitting down, she would have fallen over backward to hear so sweet and soulful a sound issuing from the depths of such a black and rugged beard. The boys, to whom this comical effect was old hat, got their amusement from watching the girls, who they knew wouldn't be able to refrain from tittering.

Tears sprang into Francie's eyes, but not from mirth. For some strange reason, Roy's peculiar singing made her inclined to cry. That high, sexless sound he produced seemed to her a bit of a marvel. Besides, it was a lovely song.

"He never spoke a word of blame," reprised Roy, "He did it just for me."

"That was Amelia's song," he said, returning to his bass boom almost as shockingly as he had left it. "Amelia is

Harvey Tuckett's wife. Well, not really. We're not sure if he had a wife or not. We're bending history a bit here. We know that Cardigan was a bit of a womanizer and we need Tuckett's grudge against his commanding officer to be emphasized. It's called dramatic licence. Also, to be honest, we're in dire need of a bit of romantic interest."

He winked as he said this at a specific point, just over Francie's head. Looking around, she saw that Isabel Archer, seated immediately behind her, was smiling discreetly back. Amelia, it seemed, was already cast.

Whereas Francie had been frankly rather jealous of the boys' plum parts, in this case she was only too relieved that hierarchy was to be properly respected. Isabel was, after all, a prefect.

"Lord Cardigan makes a pass at Amelia," went on Roy. "And Harvey Tuckett is naturally furious. That's why he takes the first opportunity to pick a fight with the earl."

An unexpected vision of jam doughnuts rose up in Francie's memory. So *that* was what the scene at the audition had been supposed to be about.

"Tuckett writes an insulting letter about Cardigan to the newspaper," went on Roy, "and Cardigan immediately challenges him to a duel. History has it that they actually met on twelfth September 1840, on Wimbledon Common."

He underlined this last sentence on the piano with a dramatic chord, as though the time, date, and place were bound to be the climax of any decent adventure story. Then without further warning he launched into another song of the rollicking Gilbert and Sullivan type, something to do with shooting people being the Englishman's favorite national sport. This time he sang in a gravelly baritone, managing to convey with a lot of eyebrow waving and head wobbling that he was a large number of people all singing at once. When he had finished, everybody clapped, and Toby began to look a bit restless.

"Who won?" called out a boy at the back.

"Won what?" said Roy, glancing at Toby.

"The duel," said the boy patiently. "Who killed who?"

"Whom," said Roy.

"Sorry," said the boy. "Whom killed who?"

"Two shots rang out," said Roy, illustrating with two loud pings on the piano, and the boys began to send him up with gasps of "ooh!" and "aah!" Roy didn't mind in the least. What teachers at Francie's school would have called cheek, he called participation.

"To no effect whatsoever," he went on teasingly. "Both men missed."

The boys groaned in chorus.

"They fired again"—ping . . . ping— "And Harvey Tuckett fell, shot through the chest."

This time even the girls joined in with the oohing and aahing.

"Luckily it was not a serious wound . . ."

The groan shook the rafters.

Toby, who had had enough of this pantomime, thought it was time they got down to some proper work. He got to his feet.

"Why don't we . . ." he began, a phrase that Francie was to come to dread, along with another favorite of his, "What if . . ." "Why don't we improvise Lord Cardigan's arrest? He was taken off to Wandsworth police station by the miller, who also happened to be a spare-time policeman. Ben, you have a go at being the miller, and Simon, you're the police inspector at the station. Joe, you be Harvey Tuckett for the time being: lie down, you're wounded. Rosanna, you can be the miller's wife—help Harvey Tuckett back to the windmill and clean up the blood. Now, who shall we have for Lord Cardigan?"

It was a question hardly worth asking. There was one person in the room suited above all others to play the rude and arrogant earl. All eyes turned to conceited Richard.

He was slow to get up. His pale, lowered eyelashes masked his expression. For a moment you might almost have imagined he was shy. It was a bit late, Francie thought, for him to start trying to pass himself off as modest. Roy beckoned him over for a private word and handed him one of his typed sheets. It appeared, to Francie's disgust, that Lord Cardigan was to have preferential treatment. While everyone else had to make up their dialogue as they went along, Richard was to be allowed to read his off the printed page.

Toby hastened to explain. There were certain things Cardigan was *known* to have said. If they stuck exactly to history where it was documented, they could afford to be as experimental as they liked elsewhere.

As soon as the boys got up to act, Francie was struck by how talented they were. Dubbs was a huge school and they were handpicked, so it was not really surprising that they were good. But up to now, sitting there so scrawny and self-conscious, they hadn't looked as though they could possibly be any use at all.

Whereas the girls all lusted to be dramatic, the boys couldn't wait to be funny. The ones with no specific part to play adopted characters of their own, and the room was suddenly teeming with old men, village idiots, and drunks. They were good at accents too; Wimbledon Common had never known so many visitors from Scotland, Ireland, and Wales. Cockney, of course, was favorite, but they were clever enough at posh voices when they wanted to be. It shook Francie a little to discover that their usual rough South London accent was as much a matter of choice as it was of chance.

Apart from Rosanna, who was busy dabbing at Harvey

Tuckett's bullet wound with a less than sterile handkerchief, the girls had nothing special to do. Francie hid herself in the crowd which followed Lord Cardigan as he was dragged off to the police station. With surprising skill, the boys conjured up a really convincing carriage, with neighing, bridling horses out in front, and rather more coachmen than necessary to whip them on. Cardigan was shunted along in the middle, impressing even Francie with the dignity of his bearing. The miller seemed to forget his prisoner was under arrest, and helped him down from the carriage as if he were a prince.

"Now then, now then, now then," began the police inspector at the station, but Richard consulted his bit of paper and interrupted him in a resonant voice that sounded to Francie like a cruel imitation of the more pompous parents of Barnes.

"I have been fighting a duel," he announced, "and I have wounded my man. Not seriously, I believe; slightly, a mere graze across the back."

Back at the windmill, Rosanna, who had been concentrating her attentions on Harvey Tuckett's front, gave him a violent push over and began applying first aid to his shoulder blades.

"Now then, now then, now then," repeated the inspector doggedly. Stifled giggles met this PC Plod characterization.

Lord Cardigan reached into a nonexistent breast pocket in his T-shirt and produced with a magician's gesture something that he flourished under the unfortunate inspector's nose. His hand was empty, but Francie, who had never seen a calling card in her life, could have sworn he was holding something small, rectangular, and white. The irritating thing was that the dreadful boy could act.

"The Earl of Cardigan," he said, clicking his heels and

drawing himself up to his full height. "Eleventh Light Dragoons."

Simon the inspector's cheeks were flaming red. He seemed about to go into his "now then, now then, now then" routine yet again, when at the last moment he came up with the only other policeman's line he had heard of: "I'm afraid I will have to take your name and address." Lord Cardigan, who had just given him them, flung him a withering look. With a glance at his script, he set about interrogating himself.

"You may ask," he said superciliously, "if I have been fighting with one of my men. And I will answer you this . . ." Fed up with police incompetence, he turned and addressed the crowd in general, reading with elaborate ceremony from his script. "Dear me, no! Do you think I would condescend to fight with one of my own officers?"

He held his head in that odd, insolent, sideways manner, looking at them with narrowed eyes over the high bridge of his nose. Heavens, how he fancied himself! Francie felt the resentment of the whole crowd welling up inside her chest.

"Put him in prison!" she said suddenly in a small, high voice.

"Yeah, shove 'im in the clink!" agreed a drunken old third-former on her right.

"Stick 'im in the nick!" called out a couple of village idiots to her left.

Then the whole crowd began yelling all at once and Harvey Tuckett, who could suffer in silence no longer, shook Rosanna off and sprang to his feet, wounded as he was, to lead the people forward in bloody revolution.

"Prison's too good for him!" he cried above the din, and the crowd began to advance on Richard like a lynch mob. What had Francie started? Busy as she was being jostled by all those tough, bony knees and elbows, and assaulted on all sides by the pungent and not altogether unpleasant smell of heated boy, it did nevertheless occur to her that Toby and Roy should stop the improvisation, *now*. But they did nothing. Perhaps they were fed up with Richard too. They let it go on until the hateful earl was on the floor with his arms pinned behind him and heroic Joe and two other boys were sitting on his head. It was only when all sense of period had flown out of the window and a couple of scary-looking skinheads started strapping Richard to an impromptu electric chair, that Roy saw fit to call a halt at last.

8

"An interesting afternoon's work," said Toby, winding up the rehearsal. *Work,* he called it! Fifteen- and sixteen-year-old boys rolling around on the floor and pretending to be horses.

"Only a bit historically inaccurate, I'm afraid. In fact, Lord Cardigan was simply bound over and allowed to leave the police station. But the anger you gave us was valuable. Ordinary people were resentful of the privileged class. A linen draper, who had committed the same offense a few months before Cardigan, was sentenced to twelve months hard labor on the treadmill. If such a thing as honor existed, why should gentlemen be free to defend it and linen drapers not?"

Why indeed. Francie could only think that if this linen draper were to be played by Richard, she would be happy to see him knocked to the ground as well.

As it was, Richard seemed quite unabashed by his punishment. He behaved as though being physically attacked was exactly the reaction he'd been trying to provoke. He got cheerfully to his feet, affectionately cuffing a small boy in glasses who had been standing on his chest. After the rehearsal had broken up, he could be seen laughing and joking with Toby and Roy, as though the three of them had set the whole thing up between them.

Communication between the sexes stopped abruptly when the acting did. As soon as they were dismissed, the girls drew back into their original corner, putting on their blazers with their backs turned. The boys started up their loudmouthed foul language again, as though to declare themselves unfit for female company. As they started pushing out through the door Roy said above the hubbub, "And if you *must* smoke, please wait till you're outside the building. If you want to get lung cancer that's your affair, but we'd rather you didn't burn the school down."

Of all the things she'd heard in the course of the afternoon, this probably shocked Francie the most. Of course, smoking went on at her own school all the time. But she had never before heard anyone in authority admit that it did. Perhaps in a school as big and wild as Dubbs, tobacco was the least of their problems. She was prepared to believe that Roy's lenient approach might make some boys less likely to bother. But when she got out into the playground, they were lighting up all over the place like glowworms in the dark.

"Like some chewing gum?" said a newly broken voice in her ear. It was Harvey Tuckett, honest Joe, wheeling his bike along with a packet of gum clutched to the handlebars. "Sugar free," he said, holding out the packet.

It seemed a surprisingly innocent offer in the face of all that nicotine.

"Thanks," said Francie, taking a piece. She was grateful for it. Despite the cold night air, her mouth was hot and dry. Rosanna, who was walking beside her, took some too. The offer, after all, had been to both of them.

"Can we have a bit?" said a fifth-former called Ruth, joining them with her friend Abigail, and soon Joe had no gum left for himself. He didn't seem to mind. The girls clamored around him, asking how old he was, what class he was in. He was fifteen and in the fourth year, just starting his general certificate exam course.

"So are we," said Ruth. "Me and Abigail, that is."

They discussed what subjects they were taking. Joe was taking ten.

"You must be bloody brainy," said Abigail. Francie noticed that girls tended to swear more when they talked to boys.

"What class are you in?" Joe asked Francie.

"Lower 4B," she answered.

"She means the second year," interpreted Ruth. "She and Rosanna are only thirteen."

Joe smiled reassuringly at Francie. "You're tall for your age," he said, which was gallant, as she wasn't, particularly.

They were outside the school gates now. Francie was relieved that there was no sign of her mother. She dreaded being seen having to be met when some people were allowed complete freedom to cycle on the main road after dark. Joe wasn't the only one. Boys on bikes were streaming down the hill, weaving their way through the heavy rush-hour traffic. At that moment all the cars approaching the school, coming up the hill on the opposite side of the road, seemed to be gray Rovers, like her mother's.

But just then Joe swung onto his saddle.

"See you next week," he said, and with a sugar-free smile, pedaled off into the night.

Francie heaved a sigh of relief and followed the other

girls to the bus stop, where she could wait as if for public transport.

"Don't you think he's handsome?" whispered Rosanna suddenly in her ear.

"Oh, *yes!*" said Francie enthusiastically, thinking how white Joe's teeth had looked in his olive-skinned face. "I really like curly hair. I suppose because mine's so straight."

"I don't mean Joe, stupid," said Rosanna scathingly. "I mean *him.*" She nodded toward a tall, shadowy figure just coming out of the school gates. Even in the failing light the careless indolence of his walk was unmistakable. It was Richard.

Francie was dumbfounded. How could anyone call a creep like that handsome? That awful sandy hair and freckled skin! That rude, haughty sideways way he stared at you! Some people had the weirdest taste. But then what else could you expect from a weirdo like Rosanna?

A horn blew right next to her and Francie jumped. Her mother's car had drawn up at the bus stop. The passenger door was open and her mother was leaning across.

"Anyone like a lift to Barnes?" she said.

To Francie's surprise, four of the girls immediately piled into the car, only too eager to be babied, quite undisgraced by the middle-class opulence of the Rover.

Only Rosanna stood back.

"Not me," she said. "My mother's meeting me off the bus at the other end."

So Francie's wasn't the only mother to fuss. Squashed in the backseat with Abigail, Ruth, and Emily, a rather fat girl from the upper fourth, Francie felt a burst of happiness to discover that the life she led was, after all, perfectly normal.

Her peace of mind didn't last long. No sooner had they set off, than her mother started firing embarrassing questions at the girls: how was the rehearsal, what did you have to do, who is playing what? As though for the price of the gas she was entitled to some insight into their lives. The girls at the back clammed up, but Isabel Archer, who sat in the front as befitted a prefect, answered quite politely for everybody. But she spoke in schoolgirl platitudes, giving nothing away. Everything was really good or really boring. The route from Wandsworth to Barnes was slow and convoluted, and the fug of the crowded car was beginning to make Francie feel sick, as was the sound of her mother's voice.

Shut up, she thought, flinging filthy looks at the rearview mirror, but her mother, not exactly a crack driver, failed to glance in it. Stuck at the traffic lights, she began to quiz Isabel about her A levels. How did her parents feel about her doing a play at the same time? Was she worried about fitting it in with all the studying she had to do? "What subjects are you doing?" she asked. "Jessica did tell me, but I've forgotten."

"English, history, and music," said Isabel. "But I'm not trying to pretend that being in a historical musical will do my exams any good. I just don't see why I can't do both."

There was an edge to her voice, and Francie could tell she was wishing she had waited for the bus.

"I'm sure you can," said Francie's mother quickly. "In fact it's probably the best thing for you. I worry about the pressure on you girls, shut up with your books night and day. You look so pale. It's getting out of proportion, this obsession with qualifications."

"Oh, *yes!*" said Isabel with feeling.

It was a pity, Francie thought, that her mother didn't take such an enlightened view when it came to Jessica.

"The thing is," said Isabel, suddenly opening up just as the journey was over, "I'd really like to go to drama school. But my parents want me to go to university. You can drop me here if you like. I live just down this road."

"I'll take you to the door. What do they want you to read?"

"History. It's what I'm supposed to be good at. But I want to be an actress."

"Be one then," said Francie's mother subversively as they drew up outside Isabel's house.

"I don't know if I'm good enough," said Isabel, sorry, now, to get out.

"You were good as Mark Antony. Anyway it's how much you want to that counts."

"Do you really think so?" said Isabel breathlessly, outside the car now but still leaning in, unable to tear herself away from such maternal wisdom. How easy it was, Francie thought, to be on the side of someone else's daughter. Almost as easy as it was to find someone else's mother more sympathetic than your own.

"Well," said Francie's mother, loath to drive away. "I expect it helps if you have a few contacts. Do you know anyone who could advise you?"

"My godfather's a producer at the BBC," said Isabel, doubtfully.

"Ask *him* then," said Francie's mother, delighted with the simplicity of the solution. Inspired by her success with young people, she ended up driving all the girls right to their front doors.

"Better not tell Daddy," said Francie, after they'd dropped the last one off miles away in Sheen. "He'll hit the roof if he thinks you've been playing chauffeur to the whole neighborhood."

Her mother giggled. For a moment it was as though they were naughty schoolgirls together. "So what were they like?" she asked as she backed the car into their own drive. "I've been dying to hear."

"Who?"

"The boys, of course."

Just in time Francie remembered that her mother was an adult, a class of person from whom such questions were not only interfering, but bordering on the kinky.

She shrugged. "All right, I suppose," she said in a bored voice. "What are we having for dinner?"

9

Francie filled in the rehearsal time on her timetable: Friday, four to six, Dubbs' Boys. Her visits to Wandsworth became a regular part of her life. She took care to remember to pack extra sandwiches on Fridays, but to drink as little as possible in case she needed to pee. It turned out that the staff lavatory was available to the girls if they were prepared to suffer the indignity of asking Roy for the key. Personally, Francie preferred to hold out if she could.

To get to Dubbs by public transport you had to change buses halfway. Francie and Rosanna traveled there together and after rehearsal someone's mother picked them up, usually Francie's own. However routine these trips became, Francie never quite got over the slightly sick headachy feeling of nerves that overtook her whenever she walked through the gates of Dubbs' School. She looked forward to it yet she dreaded it. As the evenings grew darker and colder, she envied her classmates going home on Friday afternoons to flop down in front of the television with buns and hot tea. If she had an essay as well as a lot of studying it sometimes meant that her whole weekend was up the spout. But however much homework she had, she never once considered giving up the play.

The script wasn't finished yet, so apart from learning the music, all they did for the first few weeks were games and improvisations. Francie couldn't help enjoying them, even if, as her father's child, she sometimes couldn't honestly see where they were leading. But Toby said learning to play took a lot of hard work. He said that these games were often used by professional actors to help them experience work as play. Francie liked to picture these fully grown people slaving away solemnly at Grandmother's Steps and Blind Man's Buff.

But some of the games Toby taught them were not quite so funny. There was one trick whereby you could make a person puff up with self-esteem, or fall apart in front of your eyes, just by flattering him, or treating him with contempt. Tough, bragging boys could be reduced to jelly. Francie would have liked to see Toby try it out on a girl as poised and intelligent as Isabel. But he didn't risk it, he picked on Rosanna instead, and of course she could easily be reduced to a sobbing wreck, even after she'd seen the trick tried out on several other people before her.

"We *are* the way we are treated," said Toby triumphantly, but Francie wasn't so sure. It seemed to her that Rosanna was the way *she* was for more complicated reasons.

It was at the animal game that Francie herself scored a hit. You were supposed to pretend to be an animal, but some of the boys were making a joke of it, doing Tarzan impressions and leaping up onto the furniture and scratching themselves in rude places—less interested in being monkeys than in being obscene.

"Cut out the sound effects," said Toby, "and keep the movement down to a minimum. I want you to convey to us what animal you are simply by a process of thought."

A black boy called Jed who could be very funny, lay down on the floor and was a lizard. But even lying as still as a log he couldn't resist little lizard mannerisms such as winking and poking out his tongue. Everyone was in stitches and Toby began pushing the hair out of his eyes, which was a sign that he was getting into one of his moods. Toby's moodiness was more effective than the flashes of temper most teachers went in for. By just going quiet and withdrawing his enthusiasm he could silence a roomful of delinquents in seconds.

After that, everybody tried to play the game properly, but then, of course, it got boring. People would sit or stand in the center of the room convinced that they were a rabbit or a giraffe and the poor audience would be completely baffled.

"Come on," said Toby. "Concentrate. It *can* be done."

When Francie's turn came, she decided to be Bat. It was a bit obvious, she knew, to choose a dog, but he was on her mind as he hadn't been very well lately.

She lay down on her front on the wooden floor with her legs tucked up under her to make haunches. At first she just felt rather foolishly like herself, with her chin resting on the backs of her hands and her hair, which she happened to have in looped braids that day, hanging heavily forward where Bat's droopy ears should be. But after a minute or two, the enforced silence and the lowliness and discomfort of her position began to make her feel mute and doglike and old. Old more than anything. She ached in all her bones. She preferred just to lie there. There didn't seem much point in getting up. Not even to wolf down her dinner, or strain against her lead to the park. She rolled her eyes up at an angle which showed bloodshot crescents on the undersides, hoping that someone would soon sort out for her just exactly what had gone wrong: why her legs didn't seem to support her properly, or her fur keep her warm anymore.

Suddenly in the silence of the room, Richard's voice rang out.

"She's a dying cocker spaniel," he said, in his know-all voice.

From the way Francie's nose shot up from her paws, it was obvious he had got it right. Everyone laughed, but this time it was the kind of laughter Toby approved of: a release from tension.

Francie had been so deep in her imaginings, that for a moment she thought she was upset because Richard had given her away. But then everyone started to clap and she remembered that was the point of the game: to be guessed meant you had succeeded. They were clapping for her, not Richard. She should have felt pleased, but she didn't, she felt as if she were choking. Her chest was tight and there was a terrible lump in her throat. She tried to cough and splutter the feeling away, as though she had breathed in dust with her face so close to the floor. People banged her on the back to congratulate as much as revive her. No one realized that anything real was wrong. Richard, of course, was totally unaware of the crassness of what he had said. He had said "dying." "A dying cocker spaniel." And it was true. Bat would soon die. He had to. He was too old to live much longer.

It was the first time Francie had allowed such a thought to come to the front of her mind. She knew it, but it was a shock to her. And trust Richard to be the one to point it out. To announce the imminent death of her beloved dog to a roomful of rowdy boys, and raise a cheap laugh in the process.

When she got home that evening, she rushed straight to

the kitchen to check on Bat. She was terrified after what Richard had said, he might be dead already. But he was lying in his basket and like the old gentleman he was, he hauled himself to his feet as she came into the room. She took him to his favorite place on the stairs and sat with him for a long time with her arms around his neck.

"You were brilliant at being that old dog," Joe had said to her in the playground after the rehearsal. "I bet when they announce the casting next Friday, you'll get a really good part."

But Francie felt superstitious that whatever part she got now, it would be somehow at Bat's expense. It was as though by impersonating him so accurately she had been using him up. She had made a cheap entertainment of him, paraded her private knowledge of him in public, and the better her acting, the more shame to him. Pressing her cheek against his matted fur, she was convinced that she had taken something away from him, and it was too late now to give it back.

10

Toby and Roy had been in no hurry to allocate the parts. They said they wanted to be sure, first of all, what all the members of the cast were capable of.

"We don't want to make any snap character-judgments," said Toby. "I think we proved what a dangerous game that can be on the very first day."

But the casting, when it was finally announced, followed almost exactly the pattern of that first rehearsal. Richard was to play Lord Cardigan, and Joe, Harvey Tuckett. Isabel, naturally enough, was the heroine, Amelia. Even fat Simon, who had been such a laughing stock on the first day, was to play his original part of the Police Inspector. Although she could see that their first instincts had been right, Francie couldn't help feeling a bit cheated by all the hemming and hawing that had gone on. Obviously they had made up their minds from the very beginning.

One person who *had* changed parts was Rosanna. She

had obviously made a big impression during the interven-
ing weeks and was to play Elizabeth, Lord Cardigan's
wife. Richard and Rosanna deserved each other, Francie
thought. It filled her with glee to picture Richard having
to cope with Rosanna's histrionics. Lady Cardigan was a
woman with a rather scandalous past, but according to the
script she remained, as far as Francie could tell at a glance,
entirely dry-eyed throughout the evening.

Emily, who had quite a matronly figure, was to play the
miller's wife, Mrs. Dann. Ruth and Abigail were Officers'
Wives: they weren't too pleased. They were down for
People of Putney and People in the Street as well, but
then so was everyone else.

Francie's own part was to be "Mrs. Cunningham." She
was thrilled to have a named part, even though she didn't
know who on earth Mrs. Cunningham was. She flicked
through the script, which had been handed around with
the cast list attached to it, and found that she had a de-
cent-sized scene about a third of the way through, with
quite a few lines to say. Then, on closer inspection, she
noticed to her dismay that her dialogue was almost all
with Lord Cardigan. Never mind: her character seemed
to dislike him thoroughly. Then, a few pages later, she saw
that there was a song, "Officers' wives / Lead very dull
lives," of which she was down to sing two solo verses.
Considering that some people had only one line to say, she
couldn't help feeling rather cheerful.

Joe, who was sitting next to her, gave her a commiserat-
ing look.

"What a pity you haven't got a scene with me," he said.

Toby got everyone to draw up a chair and sit in a semicircle. It was the first time they had ever been so formally
arranged. They were going to have what Toby described
as a read-through.

"We don't want any acting," he said. "Save your performances until you're up on your feet learning your moves. We want this show to grow organically. And don't, for God's sake, go home and start learning your words. They may be completely changed by next week. A play doesn't really exist on paper."

Then why bother to read it out? thought Francie. But she had to admit she was dying to hear how it sounded.

Some of the best actors were the worst readers. Boys who were confident in improvisation to the point of showing off, were suddenly quite incoherent in the face of the written word. What with all the mumbling and stuttering, Francie found it hard to concentrate. There were moments of great clarity where Isabel read, or Richard had a long speech, but on the whole she was hard pushed to follow the plot at all. There seemed to be two officers in Lord Cardigan's regiment, both called Captain Reynolds. The bigger of the two parts, Captain Richard Reynolds, was to be played by the black, lizard boy, Jed, who had turned out to have a remarkably good singing voice. His namesake, Captain John Reynolds, an officer much picked upon by Lord Cardigan, was to be played by a boy called Hamish, not a very good actor but the only other black member of the cast.

This slightly symbolic piece of casting worried Francie, especially as the two persecuted officers had a song: "He Can't Tell the One from the Other." She was busy combing the script for other racially suspect material when suddenly Toby's voice shouted, "Mrs. Cunningham, Mrs. Cunningham!" and she realized she had missed her cue. She looked up with flaming cheeks to find Richard glaring at her across the semicircle, waiting for her to speak. She fumbled around with the pages, trying to find the place, and eventually dropped her script on the floor. Joe shoved his script under her nose, pointing out the place. She read out her lines flatly, with her eyes glued to the page. At least no one could accuse her of acting. She hadn't a clue, anyway, what her character was meant to convey.

But lying in bed that evening, reading through her lines and trying not to memorize them, she was pleased to find that there was quite a lot she could do with this Mrs. Cunningham. She was a bitchy, gossipy society woman who started the rumor that led directly to the duel between Cardigan and Tuckett. Francie was glad to be instrumental in Lord Cardigan's downfall, although she wished Harvey Tuckett had been a better shot. She fell asleep in the middle of reading, and had a rather embarrassing dream in which things really had gone differently and Joe had fatally wounded Richard. Rosanna was kneeling over Richard's dead body, sobbing and screaming curses. The lynch mob was descending on Joe and Francie was trying to fend them off with her bare hands. Joe put his arm around her to protect her, but when she turned around he had changed identity again and become Richard, leering into her face. Her fear of the mob was nothing to the menace of those prickly white eyelashes, which came so close to her she could feel them like insects' legs walking on her cheeks. She tried to scream but no sound came out: he was blocking out her source of light and air.

She awoke to discover that she was indeed being smothered: by her script, which had fallen over her nose.

Jessica was in love. It was obvious just to look at her. She had a daft, moony expression and changed her clothes even more often than usual. The object of her affection was a young man in his third year at art college, whom Francie had only met in the dark at the front door.

"I'm not bringing him in," said Jessica, "to have him inquisitioned by Dad about his attitude to twentieth-century painting. And you know what Mum's like."

Mum was like a mother in a high old state about her daughter. What worried her was not that Jessica would go to bed with the boy, but that she would ride on the back of his motorbike.

"It's a *mo*ped, Mum," said Jessica. "It goes about five miles an hour. And it only seats one. When he takes me out we go on foot."

But Francie's mother would not be comforted. When Jessica was out, she would rush to the window every time an engine revved in the street.

"I caught her snooping in my bedroom the other day," said Jessica privately to Francie. "Any decent mother would have been looking for contraceptive pills. But she was peering under the bed. I think she must have been hunting for a crash helmet."

"Would she have found any?" said Francie. She spoke softly for fear of jolting Jessica into remembering it was her boring little sister she was talking to.

"Any what?"

"Any what you said. Pills."

Jessica blushed and looked mysterious.

"I've got a prescription," she said. "But I haven't taken it to the chemist yet."

"Are you going to?"

"What?"

"Take it to the chemist."

"I expect so."

"When?"

"Soon. Don't tell Mum. I'm sure she thinks I've been Doing It for ages. It's the thought of her guessing that puts me off."

"Don't worry," said Francie. "We don't have those sorts of conversations much these days. She hasn't told me the facts of life for ages. She's given up on me because I haven't got my curse yet."

"Tell me when you do," said Jessica, putting her arm around her little sister. "I'll sort you out." There were times when it was just possible to imagine Jessica as a doctor.

At other times imagination boggled. Sometimes she screamed at Francie to get out of her room.

"I'm studying," she would shriek, although in fact she was lying flat on her back on her bed, without a textbook in sight. Love seemed to have made her more full of hate than ever. It was Christmastime, and the explosive atmosphere she created in the house threatened to shatter the fragile glass balls on the Christmas tree. Francie didn't know how they were going to get through Christmas Day, what with Bat so poorly and Jessica moping to be with her boyfriend. She felt sad that she wasn't excited in the way she used to be when she was little. When the big day arrived, she didn't wake up at the crack of dawn and hover outside her parents' bedroom door, giggling and clearing her throat until the whole household was disturbed. She felt lazy and sleepy as on any ordinary day and had to be shouted at and nagged to get up.

But despite a late start, Christmas went off rather well. Francie's grandmother came to lunch, and everyone pulled themselves together for her sake. Even Bat had quite a revival of spirits and romped around in the piles of discarded wrapping paper like a puppy. Aware that it was likely to be his last Christmas, Francie's father refrained from cries of "Get that bloody dog out of here."

After lunch everyone, except Francie's grandmother, who fell asleep, played a game of Trivial Pursuit, which Francie had just been given. Jessica, who was very competitive, won by miles, which cheered her up and stopped her listening for the telephone. Francie caused quite a stir by knowing the answer to a history question: "Who led the Charge of the Light Brigade?" Her parents were on good form, with her father getting the answers wrong on purpose and her mother getting them right by mistake. Bat snored away under the table and Francie felt rather tipsy from all the brandy in the plum pudding. Looking around from one face to another—from her frowning, vivacious sister, to her astute, vague-eyed mother, to her bossy, beaming father—Francie couldn't avoid the sneaking suspicion that she belonged to what is commonly known as a Happy Family.

But the very next day she heard an awful sobbing sound

coming from Jessica's room. She stood outside the door, rooted to the spot, afraid to go in for fear of being shouted at. Francie had never heard her sister cry quite like that before. What had happened? Jessica had been out for most of the day with her boyfriend, Matthew. Perhaps they had Done It and it had gone wrong. Curiosity got the better of Francie. She turned the handle quietly and went in.

No wonder the sound had seemed strange. It wasn't Jessica crying at all. It was Isabel Archer, sitting on the floor, sobbing her heart out. Jessica was standing by the window with her right hand clapped behind her back. There was a strong smell of smoke in the room.

Francie was annoyed with everyone. She was annoyed with Jessica for wanting to be a doctor at the same time as filling her lungs with disgusting black sludge. She was annoyed with her parents for forbidding Jessica to smoke, thereby making her more impatient to puff away behind their backs than she was to climb into bed with her boyfriend. Most of all she was annoyed with Isabel for coming to her house to cry. Cool, beautiful Isabel, whom Toby and Roy, with all their clever tricks, had never succeeded in ruffling, had no business to be sitting hunched up on Jessica's grotty floor with her face all red and blotchy. Isabel belonged to the private world of Dubbs' Boys. It unnerved Francie to come across her unexpectedly like this, out of context and out of character. She wanted to rush up to her and put her arm around her and ask what was the matter, as she would have done at rehearsal, but she couldn't with Jessica staring at her with that stupid, hateful, cross-eyed, caught-out look.

As soon as Jessica saw that it wasn't a parent or a teacher who had just burst in, but only ineffectual little Francie who would never tell, she took her hand from behind her back and flicked ash onto the floor.

"Don't just stand there," she said impatiently. "Can't you see Isabel's upset? Piss off. And shut the door behind you."

"Piss off yourself," said Francie, but she went. Hours later, after Isabel had left, she swallowed her pride and went back to Jessica's room to try to find out what was going on.

Jessica looked up from her desk with a virtuous smile, only too happy to be interrupted now that she really was studying.

"I'm sorry, darling, I can't tell you. She was just upset, that's all."

"It must have been something important. You were talking for ages. Is it something to do with the play? Has Toby or Roy been horrid to her?"

"It's a private problem of Isabel's. Nothing to do with you."

"But Isabel is to do with me," said Francie stubbornly. "We're in the play together."

Jessica got up and crossed the room, which was unusually tidy, and put her arm around Francie.

"I'm not being mean," she said kindly. "I *would* tell you, honestly, only I promised Isabel not to say anything. She doesn't want anyone to know until she's sure what's going to happen. Hey, I've got a great new record. Want to hear it?"

Francie pushed her sister's arm off and turned sharply away.

"I don't know how Matthew can stand it," she said.

"Stand what?" said Jessica nervously. It was easy to get a rise out of her if you mentioned Matthew.

Francie turned as she reached the door. "You coming close to him," she said coldly. "Your breath reeks of smoke."

12

After a fortnight's separation over the Christmas holidays, the cast of *An Affair of Honor* were overjoyed to see one another again. It was amazing, Francie thought, what a sense of comradeship had been built up in the few weeks they'd been rehearsing the play. Of course, she was pleased to see her own schoolfriends as well, after the break, but she didn't particularly look forward to the new term's work, and she and Amanda greeted each other on the first freezing day of term with a sigh as well as a smile. But at Dubbs it was all unalloyed pleasure. Boys and girls who had been so standoffish only a couple of months ago flung their arms around each other's necks as though they were lifelong friends. Due to the overwhelming number of boys per girl, Francie had quite a few personal admirers. It was easy enough to hug the ones she knew *didn't* fancy her. But going into a clinch with the ones she thought maybe *did,* was more of a problem. Where Joe was concerned, for instance, she felt particularly shy, and stood with her arms stiffly by her side when he finally worked his way around to her. But he was not to be denied and planted a hot, hard kiss close to her left ear, which made her feel for the rest of the afternoon that one cheek was redder than the other. Mind you, by the time he'd finished saying hello, she wasn't the only girl with a lopsided complexion.

Richard strolled languidly up to her, twisting the corners of his mouth in what she supposed must be meant to be a smile. For one awful moment she thought that he was going to go into the hugging routine as well. But he merely tweaked her pigtail and passed by. Francie's scalp prickled with indignation. She'd been toying with the idea of having her hair cut short and she decided then and there that the time had come for drastic action.

What with all the excitement of seeing the boys again, Francie didn't notice at first that Isabel was missing from the rehearsal. She'd seen her earlier, at school, reading the lesson in assembly, so it couldn't be that she was ill. When it came to Amelia's first bit with Harvey Tuckett, the whole scene had to be passed over, and rumors started to fly.

"Isabel's not coming back."

"She's dropped out of the play."

"Her parents have made her give it up because of her A levels."

"There's been a terrible row."

"Toby and Roy are really upset."

So was Francie. She couldn't imagine the play without Isabel. So far the scenes they'd rehearsed were just fragments, meaningless bits of a jigsaw picked up and tried out at random. But whenever Isabel got up to act, you could suddenly get a glimpse of the whole picture. She'd already made a character of Amelia, a cool-headed self-possessed young woman, charmingly uncorrupted by all the male intrigue around her. Her singing of "Just for Me," had promised to be the musical high spot of the evening. Then there was the example she set: the seriousness of her attitude, her perfect, prefect behavior. Francie felt even sorrier for Toby and Roy than she did for Isabel.

But they both carried on as though nothing had happened. Perhaps they believed their own propaganda about not needing stars. Everyone making an equal contribution and so on. But who, thought Francie, among the remaining girls could possibly make a contribution equal to Isabel's? Rosanna was probably the best actress among them, but apart from being too young to play the main part, she was too outlandish for a Victorian heroine. Perfect for the extravagant, temperamental Lady Cardigan, she was all wrong for Amelia. Neither Ruth nor Abigail were good enough at singing to carry a big number by themselves. And Emily was frankly too fat. There was nothing for it. Toby and Roy would just have to go back to the girls' school and look again.

The rehearsal ended ten minutes earlier than usual. Toby and Roy withdrew to the far end of the room, talking earnestly together. They must be more worried than they'd let on. Francie racked her brains as to who in the sixth form could possibly take over the part. There were lots of good people who hadn't gone to the audition in the first place, who might be persuaded to step in. Of course, everyone knew that the best actress in the school apart from Isabel was her own sister, Jessica. Francie was suddenly convinced that the next thing she knew, Toby and Roy would be stirring up more family trouble by asking Jessica to audition.

And sure enough, as she picked up her bag to go, Toby called out, "Frances, can you spare us a moment?"

Crossing the room, she quickly tried to prepare a speech about Jessica's A levels being every bit as important as Isabel's: more so, if anything, as she wanted to be a doctor. She was about to launch into it, when Roy said in a voice as discreet as his boom would allow, "Can you just hang on for a minute, Frances? We'd like to try you out for the part of Amelia."

There was a loud, thumping noise in Francie's head. Her heart seemed to be operating up there where her wits should have been. She shifted her openmouthed stare to Toby, so that he could quickly correct what Roy had said, or give her the wink that it was just a joke. But they were both looking at her with the same bright, unblinking, slightly sinister smile. For a moment they ceased to be two people at all and became one four-eyed monster: thick and thin Toby-and-Roy who could turn unsuspecting little girls into leading ladies. She was horribly in the creature's power.

"But I'm too young," she said when she could speak. "There are people in higher classes . . ."

"There's no class prejudice here," said Roy in amusement. "Being the right age isn't as important as having the right quality."

"I'm not a bit like Isabel," protested Francie, but her resistance was flagging. It wasn't just Toby and Roy she was fighting, but her own surging, swelling desire to have a go.

"We're not looking for another Isabel," said Toby impatiently. "We're looking for a new Amelia. Let's just see how the reading goes, shall we? First things first."

Francie could see Ruth and Abigail whispering together as they put on their coats. They could see what was happening. It was obvious from their faces they thought her a right little upstart.

For some reason their resentment gave her courage. She ran after Rosanna, who was just going out of the door.

"If you see my mother, tell her to wait," she said. "Say

I'll be down in a few minutes. I've got to try out for Amelia."

"Okay," said Rosanna breezily. That was one nice thing about Rosanna. She never had normal reactions, such as jealousy.

The scene Francie was to read was with Joe, but Richard took it upon himself to stay back as well. She could have done without his interfering presence. While she was given time to look through Amelia's lines, he stood at the other end of the room, just out of earshot, deep in discussion with Toby and Roy, as though he wasn't a member of the cast at all but actually one of the staff. The three of them appeared to be having a heated argument about her. Francie buried her nose in the script, but her ears kept tuning in to the odd word that floated across the room. From time to time Richard's haughty voice rose above the low buzz of the others.

"Too young . . ." she heard him say. "Not fair . . ." So he really was against her. She hadn't just imagined he was her enemy. Of *course* there were people older and more deserving than she was. But why shouldn't she have a chance? What had he got against her? He kept glancing in her direction as he spoke, his face red with annoyance. Obviously he was determined she shouldn't have the part. Her father had been right when he'd said what a ruthless, competitive place the theater was. But what did Richard have to be competitive about? He already had the best part in the play. He must just think she wasn't good enough. Well, she would show him. She would show them all.

"Want to read it through with me?" said Joe at her elbow, but Toby was already advancing down the room toward her.

"Let's worry about all that after we've cast the part," he said over his shoulder to Richard and Roy. "We haven't even auditioned her yet. Are you ready Frances? In your own time."

To her surprise, Francie found that she didn't have to refer to the script at all. That early instruction, that they were on no account to learn their lines, had ensured that within the space of a few rehearsals everyone else's lines as well as her own were engraved on her memory. She and Joe played the scene where Amelia tells her husband how happy she is to have escaped Lord Cardigan's attentions.

"God knows, he is a cruel, scheming fellow!" she was able to cry out with a true vengeance.

Joe gave her every support. He held her hand tightly and gazed at her with feeling as he explained that he had given up his career in the army for her sake. Francie was so transported by the blueness of his eyes that when Roy tentatively picked out the opening chords of "Just for Me" on the piano, she launched without hesitation into the song.

This was the bit she'd been dreading. Isabel had such a strong, mature singing voice: how could she possibly compete? But strangely, as she sang, Francie's memory leapt straight over the shining example of Isabel's vibrating tones and flew back to an earlier, quainter rendition of the song: Roy's first, high-pitched interpretation of his own composition. It was to his plaintive falsetto that she tried to match her own husky, oddly boyish voice.

"He did it just for me," she sang, looking Richard straight in the eye, using her hatred of him to invest the song with a rather startlingly passionate note of irony,

> "Though I never asked him to,
> Though his life would never be the same,
> He never spoke a word of blame,
> He did it just for me."

There was a long silence when she'd finished. As a sort of afterthought Francie blushed a deep, dark red. Unable to keep her eyes on Richard's face when she wasn't performing, she nevertheless had the fleeting impression that his fierce look had softened. Toby and Roy were clearly impressed; not so much, Francie thought, with her performance, as with their own clever perception in predicting she could do it. They began to talk loudly to each other as though she wasn't there.

"I think we might be off the hook here, with a bit of luck."

"I don't mind the rawness in the voice—there's quite a lot of resonance."

"She's not very tall, I know, but with all that hair piled up . . ."

"I'm having my hair cut short quite soon," said Francie, to remind them she was listening.

"Don't," said Toby sharply. "We need it the way it is!" and that, apparently, was that. Since her hair now seemed to belong to them, was she to take it that the part was hers, in exchange? She waited for a more formal announcement, but none came.

Richard tapped his foot impatiently and then suddenly strode across the room and patted Francie, of all things, on the head.

"You did well, little Fran," he said quietly. "Too well, I'm afraid. I can't really blame them for taking advantage of you. Congratulations."

What a hypocrite! To congratulate her now, after all he had said against her! Really, the boy was the limit. But despite the outrageous things he had called her, "little" again, and "Fran," just for a moment she had the strange sensation that she liked him. It must have been what he was telling her. She was going to play Amelia. It really was true. She had heard of messengers being punished purely for the bad news they brought. Perhaps it worked in reverse. Perhaps it was impossible not to feel a rush of warmth for your worst enemy if the news you were brought was brilliant.

"People don't call me Fran," she said. "They call me Francie."

She had meant it to be a rebuff, but it came out like an invitation to call her by her pet name. Luckily, Joe came to her rescue.

"If you get here early next week," he said, "I'll take you through our other scenes before rehearsal starts. We'll be really good together. You'll see."

Francie walked out through the deserted playground in a daze. She'd completely forgotten that her mother must have been sitting outside the school waiting for her all this time.

But it wasn't her mother who'd come today. It was her father. She walked right past his sports car before she realized whose it was.

"Where the hell did you get to?" he said angrily. "I suppose you keep your mother waiting like this every week. All the others came out twenty minutes ago."

"I had to stay back," said Francie. "They wanted to hear me sing. Isabel's left the play and I've been given the main part."

"So I should bloody well think," said her father. "There's no point in trailing all the way down here every Friday for anything less. Put your seat belt on quickly, I've got to get back to look after the dinner."

"Where's Mum?" said Francie, suddenly frightened, suddenly seeing that a school play was only a school play.

Her father revved the engine.

"Poor old Bat's taken a turn for the worse," he said. "Your mother's had to take him to the vet."

13

The vet gave Bat a reprieve this time. But she said that his lungs were in pretty poor shape and she doubted if he would make it through the winter.

"We may have to make the decision ourselves," said Francie's mother. "The day will come soon when we'll have to be prepared to give Bat up for his own sake."

She meant put him in the car, drive him to the vet, and hand him over for execution. How could anyone in the family bring themselves to do such a thing? He would know, Francie was sure. He was no fool. He hated the vet. When he was taken there, even for something minor, he began to tremble as soon as he got in the car. Perhaps he had an instinct that one day he wouldn't be coming back. Francie had a new and horrible fear: that it would be from the look on *her* face that he'd know when his hour of doom had come.

Sometimes she felt guilty that she could so easily forget his troubles. Now that she was playing Amelia, rehearsals at Dubbs absorbed her more than ever. She made a great show of doing her homework so that her parents wouldn't think her schoolwork had been affected. But her report before Christmas had not been good. "Rather scatter-brained," "Doesn't concentrate," "Always in a dream." It was true. She *was* always dreaming. And more often than not, her dream was to do with the play. While the math mistress rabbited on about quadratic equations, Francie would go over and over her lines in her head, trying to make them ring true. How would it feel to be a young Victorian woman, unable to speak out for herself, waiting and worrying at home while men shot at each other to protect her honor? Would it be exciting and romantic? Or would she be overcome by fear? Maybe she would suspect her husband of picking this quarrel to settle old scores of his own. Francie wrote the word *Amelia* in different hand-writing all over the page of her math book, as though by inventing her signature, a real person might come to life. She tried to find some modern parallel for Amelia's pre-dicament, but the only behavior model she could come up with was her mother. The sort of twittering anxiety *she* displayed when she imagined Jessica was being raped on the common, seemed a bit exaggerated for the stage. An old-fashioned heroine would be more stoical, Francie was sure. But dueling was a serious business, leading if not to death at least to injury and imprisonment. How would I feel, she thought, humming to herself, if someone were prepared to take such a risk Just for Me? Secretly she'd be a bit flattered, she had to admit. But she'd be angry too. Angered and frustrated, as women have been down the centuries, at the childish, dangerous idiocy of men.

Amanda, who in the old days would have been glad to cough up several pence for her thoughts, knew better than to waste her money. You could bet your bottom dollar that Francie was thinking about Dubbs. Amanda and Sarah agreed that the subject was becoming a bore. They were great buddies now, those two. Not getting into the play had created a bond between them. Lately they were always giggling away at private jokes and passing notes to each other over Francie's head. Francie found herself drifting away from her old set of friends and eating her sandwiches with Rosanna. There was so much to discuss. Of all the girls in the cast, Rosanna had been the only one to be really nice about the business of Francie's taking over Amelia. Abigail hadn't been too bitchy, since she'd inherited the part of Mrs. Cunningham. But Emily and Ruth had been cows. They'd gone around saying that success had changed Francie. Francie disagreed. As far as she could see, the only effect of her success so far had been to change *them.*

Rosanna, on the other hand, seemed genuinely pleased for her.

"I think you'll be just as good as Isabel in your own way," she said. "Would you like to stay the night at my house next Friday?"

Rosanna lived in quite a large house in Putney. On the outside it was the same sort of size and age as Francie's, but it couldn't have been more different inside.

The walls of the rooms in Francie's house were all plain white—"As a background to the pictures," her parents were fond of saying. But the walls of Rosanna's house were like pictures in themselves, covered in dark, exotic patterned wallpapers and fabrics. There were mirrors and trick lighting effects everywhere, and Francie kept thinking there was another room beyond when there wasn't. None of the alterations seemed to be quite finished.

"We're painting this ceiling blood red," said Rosanna, taking Francie through a room where all the furniture stood around swathed in sheets, like ghosts. Another room had no ceiling at all. "We're turning it into a conservatory," said Rosanna.

Francie was used to arriving home from rehearsal to the smell of cooking, but with all this transformation going on here, there didn't seem much prospect of a hot meal.

"Mum and I are vegetarians," explained Rosanna, but there were no vegetables in the house either. Rosanna and Francie were allowed to go out and buy whole-wheat pizzas and eat them on their laps in front of any television program they liked. Several Siamese cats stalked about the house, sleek, haughty, and uninterested in food, like Rosanna herself. Glamorous though they were, they were somehow not the kind of creatures you could make friends with. Much as she loved animals, Francie couldn't really find it in her heart to want to pick them up and put them on her lap and stroke them.

At one point in the evening, Rosanna's mother, who seemed to be under a lot of personal pressure, went out for a while and left the girls alone in the house. Rosanna immediately opened a can of beer and put a sexy foreign film on the video and fast-forwarded to the bit where the actors took off their clothes.

Francie was impressed with Rosanna's life-style, although she didn't much like the taste of the beer and couldn't take her eyes off the action long enough to catch the gist of the subtitles. There was nothing she liked better than glossy sex scenes in American movies between young, tanned, athletically gifted people. But these two roly-poly, middle-aged Europeans grunting and heaving about in black and white and flashing their unexpectedly hairy armpits made her feel a bit queasy.

"I feel really sorry for those poor actors," she said. "They probably hardly know each other. Imagine having to do a scene like that with a boy at Dubbs. Do you think they're just simulating? Or do they really have to Do It?"

"I've heard there are some films where they really Do," said Rosanna darkly. "Sometimes the actors can't stop themselves. Or else the director insists."

"I bet Toby and Roy would insist," said Francie, giggling, and Rosanna started to imitate Toby's voice: "I want it real."

"No faking!" they both shouted, and fell off the sofa in stitches, spilling foamy beer all over the carpet. The strange thing was that Rosanna's mother, who chose that moment to walk in the front door, didn't seem at all put out by what went on behind her back. She smiled at them indulgently, as though suddenly remembering she was supposed to be a mother, and offered them some chocolate. Lighting a cigarette for herself, she was inclined to settle down and watch the rest of the film with them. Francie, who automatically assumed that all adults who smoked must be seriously unhappy, thought she looked as though she could do with some company. But Rosanna had no intention of including her mother in their revels. They were going upstairs, she said, to wash their hair.

"I'm not," said Francie. "Mine takes too long to dry." But Rosanna was determined. She insisted on shampooing Francie's hair so that she could make dozens of little thin braids all over her head and leave them to dry overnight.

"It'll look brilliant," she said, blow-drying her own short hair in seconds. "It'll come out all crinkly in the morning."

Rosanna went in for beauty treatments on a grand scale. Before the evening was out, she and Francie had mud-packed their faces, manicured their nails, and strip-waxed their legs. The hairs on Francie's legs were quite fine and fair; she'd never really noticed them before. But Rosanna said they were gross: no boy would be able to bear to touch them. She showed Francie how to apply the plastic strips and rip them off sharply, like adhesive tape.

"Scream as you do it," she advised, with a piercing demonstration. "The louder you scream, the less it hurts."

Scream or no scream, Francie found it hurt like crazy. The pain seemed hardly worth it on the off chance that a boy might graze his hand in passing on her ankle.

"Hadn't we better pack this in?" she said. "It's past midnight. If we keep up this racket your mother will come in and start nagging us to go to bed."

"No, she won't," said Rosanna. "I'm allowed to go to sleep as late as I like."

She was allowed to draw on the walls as well. She'd recently moved bedrooms and the walls of her new room had been left the pink, sludgy color of plaster for her to scribble on as the mood took her. There were felt-tipped-pen graffiti all over the place. It was like living inside the pages of someone's private diary. I HATE YOU was written in large red letters over the bed and then crossed out. After she saw that, Francie tried not to read any more intimate messages. She was sure they must all be addressed to Rosanna's father. There was a photograph of him, or what she took to be him, tucked into the frame of Rosanna's mirror, looking rather handsome and surprisingly butch, but not very cheerful, for a gay person. Rosanna saw her looking at it and said enigmatically, "I'm never going to get married, are you?"

Contrary to expectation Rosanna's mother did burst in, ghostly in an antique nightie, shouting at them in a hysterical voice to get to bed at once. Francie was rather relieved to be bossed about. She was beginning to find Rosanna's freedom a bit oppressive. Friday was a long day, what with school being followed so closely by rehearsal. Despite her uncomfortable wet braids she was sure she'd fall asleep as soon as her head hit the pillow.

But turning off the lights was only a beginning. Rosanna was determined to talk till dawn. And what she wanted to talk about was boys. For someone who was never going to get married she took an unnaturally healthy interest in the opposite sex.

For a start, she knew everyone at Dubbs miles better than Francie did. She seemed to have spent her time at rehearsals sizing up every boy in the play.

"He's such a love," she would say. "A real babe, don't you think?"

Or: "He's revolting, he really disgusts me."

"He's got a few spots," Francie would agree.

"Oh," said Rosanna, who loved to shock, "it's not *that*. I can be really attracted to bad skin. Zits can be a real turn-on on the right boy."

"Can they?" said Francie in astonishment. She was lying on a camp bed, close to the floor, and Rosanna's voice, floating down from the bed above, seemed full of lofty and superior knowledge.

"Take Zach," said Rosanna, referring to a rather frightening-looking boy with a Mohawk hairdo. "I really go for him. All those wonderful pockmarks."

Pockmarks apart, Francie couldn't have been more amazed. Zach was the kind of boy whose idea of chatting up a girl was to get her on the floor with her arms twisted behind her back.

"He's a bit rough," she said doubtfully.

"I suppose your idea of a sexy-looking boy is Joe," said Rosanna scornfully.

Francie was beginning to doubt the wisdom of this visit. But she was too intrigued by what Rosanna would say next, not to answer.

"Well," she said. "I do quite like him. He gives me a lot of confidence when I act with him."

"God, what an obvious choice," said Rosanna. "*Everyone* fancies him. And he knows it. He's always around the back of the lavatories, getting off with anything in a skirt he can lay his hands on."

"How do *you* know?" said Francie crossly. She was getting a bit sick of Rosanna and her inside information. What did she say about *her* when she wasn't there?

"He's a member of the Battersea Rude Boys," said Rosanna airily. "Surely you must know who *they* are."

Francie didn't have a clue, but she took a stab in the dark.

"The Rude Boys are really old-fashioned," she said. "*Nobody* belongs to them anymore."

"Well," said Rosanna hastily, "anyway. He lives down on a really grotty housing estate in Battersea. He hangs around with a gang of awful yobs."

"Living in welfare housing doesn't make a person a yob," said Francie disapprovingly. "Anyway, I don't believe he's like that at all. He's taking ten subjects for GCSE."

There was a creak of springs as Rosanna rolled over and lolled her head comically over the side of the bed.

"Taking ten GCSEs doesn't make a person a saint, either," she said, giggling. "Don't believe me if you don't want to. You'll find out."

"If you think you're putting me off him, you're not," said Francie fiercely. She could hardly expect Rosanna to understand that to a person of her upbringing, finding out that Joe came from a poor background only made him seem more romantic than ever. Lecherous, wild, *and* disadvantaged—her mother would make her invite him home to tea on the spot.

"There's no need to be so touchy," said Rosanna, settling down again, "I'm only telling you for your own good. It's not as though I want him for myself, or anything. Anyway, he can't be your real Obsession. You're just saying him to put me off the scent. I know there's someone else in your love life. Come on. Own up."

Rosanna had stuck dozens of luminous stars to her ceiling, which glowed in the dark. Francie stared up at them, dredging her mind for someone to satisfy her friend's feverish imagination. It seemed too foolish to admit that when she went to Dubbs, her real Obsession was the play.

"I like Jed quite a lot," she said at last. "He really makes me laugh." She picked on Jed because he was black and she wanted to give Rosanna something to think about. And he *was* rather hunky as the persecuted Captain Reynolds. "I could listen to him sing all day," she said.

"Who couldn't?" said Rosanna, not to be outdone. "I wouldn't mind finding myself trapped in the back row of Putney cinema with him. He's got a great body. Ruth thinks so too. Have you seen the looks she gives him in rehearsal? But you could get him away from her. All the boys want to get off with you now you're playing the main part. I'll tell him you fancy him if you like. That always gets men going."

"No!" said Francie in alarm. "Don't do that! I didn't say I fancied him. Ruth can have him. Don't tell *her* what I said. She hates me enough as it is."

"Don't worry," said Rosanna, "I was only teasing. She wouldn't believe me anyway. Everyone knows who you really fancy."

"Who-oo?" said Francie, breathing out the word in wonderment like an owl. Her earlobes, cold from her wet hair, were suddenly burning, the way they're supposed to when people have been gossiping about you.

"Oh, come *on*," said Rosanna. "You really are a close one, aren't you. Mind you, I don't blame you. I think he's gorgeous. He gives me a real womb-wave every time I see him. But unfortunately he's never looking at me. He's always got his eyes on you."

"Who-oo-oo?" said Francie again, on three urgent, descending notes this time. Rosanna's insinuations were beginning really to upset her.

"You mean to tell me you really don't know?" said Rosanna disbelievingly. "Richard, of course, who else? My husband, the famous Lord Cardigan."

Francie sat up so that she could see Rosanna's face.

"You're mad," she said furiously, "as mad as people say you are. I loathe Richard, as it happens. And he loathes me. He tried to stop me getting Amelia if you want to know. He's one of the few people I've ever really hated in my life."

Rosanna starting laughing at Francie's braids, which as they dried were beginning to spring out from her head like wires.

"You do look funny," she said. "If Richard could see you now, I might stand a chance. Anyway, if you're not attracted to him, how come you're getting so upset?"

Francie was speechless with fury. Rosanna tossed about in her antique brass bed, pretending to get comfortable. When she spoke again, it was in a different, thicker voice.

"Since when did you have to like someone to fancy them, anyway?" she said bitterly. "Everyone knows that's all just romantic slush. Have you ever seen two cats mating? I saw mine once. The female screams the place down. They hiss and scratch as though they really want to kill each other. Sex hasn't got anything to do with love. If it did have, people wouldn't be in the kind of trouble they are."

Somehow Francie knew that this conversation led all the way back to the subject of Rosanna's father, and she couldn't get into all *that* now. But she couldn't be angry anymore, either.

"Let's go to sleep," she said, settling her bumpy head

back on her damp pillow. "We can go on talking in the morning. I don't know about you, but I'm knackered."

"Spoilsport," said Rosanna, but in the silence that followed it was she who dropped straight off to sleep. Francie lay awake for a long time, staring up at the luminous stars until their painted radiance gave out and they faded away into darkness.

14

For a while, rehearsing seemed to be an end in itself. There was no right or wrong way to play a scene: only an endless stream of possibilities, any one of which might lead off in a new and interesting direction.

"Let's stop and re-imagine this," Toby would say. "I wonder what would happen if we approached this from another point of view."

But at the beginning of February he began to take a more practical tone.

"That's your spot," he started to shout, "stick to it."

"Don't do that, you're holding up the action."

"We can't go over it again, we must press *on*."

What was not right would have to go on as it was. The countdown to the opening night had begun.

Friday afternoon sessions moved into the theater. It wasn't just a hall with a platform at one end, as at Francie's school. It had a proper, functional stage with wings and flies. The seats in the small auditorium rose in tiers. Of course, they were hardly plush velvet, but who cared. Francie loved the dusty, workmanlike atmosphere, the stuffy blacked-out nighttime that existed here in the middle of the afternoon. The scenery had been built and painted by the boys from the art and woodwork classes, and it was a revelation. At last there were real stairs to go up and down, doors that opened and closed.

Some people found reality inhibiting. Actors who could mime turning a door handle perfectly well came over completely uncoordinated on the set. And some performances suffered in the transition. Scenes that had been lively and effective in the intimacy of the rehearsal room looked suddenly dull and dwarfed on the stage. Delicate emotions did not always carry. Crass overstatements often did.

"Speak up!" shouted Toby from the back of the auditorium. "Look out front when you say that—we can't see your face. Can't you make that gesture a bit bigger? For God's sake, *project*!"

The big singing numbers were in chaos. The school orchestra had been brought in and the violins were scraping away at a different tempo from the chorus. There was much cursing as soldiers collided with policemen pushing their way in opposite directions through the narrow wings. Francie felt completely disorientated. She had a dreadful cold and could hardly speak, let alone sing.

"He did it just for be," she croaked, patting her throat in the hope that Toby and Roy would realize she had health problems. But there was no such thing as sympathy in the theater.

"It's not good enough," bellowed Roy from the orchestra pit. "This show will never be ready in four weeks' time. It's a physical impossibility."

"Don't take it personally," said Joe as Francie hurried off into the wings to blow her nose. But with acting there was no other way to take it. When it was no good, it was *you* who failed: your face, your voice, your whole personality. What if she were to have a cold on the actual night? She could hardly put up her hand and say to the audience, excuse me, my nose is blocked up, my throat hurts, if you don't mind I'd rather go home to bed. You had to give them their money's worth. Anything less was cheating.

Extra rehearsals were called. They were to go in all day for the next two Sundays, and the Sunday after that was the dress rehearsal.

When she first saw her costume, Francie didn't like it at all. She was envious of Rosanna's, which was a wonderful rich burgundy color, made of silky stuff, with a swanky bonnet to match. All the officers' wives had prettier dresses than she did. Hers was made of dull, limp gray stuff and was the plainest of all in design. When she went for her first fitting, she could have cried.

"Are you sure this is the right one?" she said as the mothers who were doing the sewing tugged and pushed at her petticoats. She gazed with envy at the other dresses hanging on the rack, with their bright stripes and frilled flounces. "Don't I even have a hat?"

"No," said the head mother, consulting her list and showing Francie a drawing of the way her hair was to be done: in loops over her ears and knotted on the top of her head. "Don't worry, dear. It'll look very Victorian."

"Never mind Victorian," said Francie anxiously. "Will it suit me?"

The woman fitting her bodice got a bit rough with the pins.

"Ouch!" said Francie, and the mothers smiled. It was obvious they thought her a proper little madam.

Francie's fitting was on a Tuesday, and because it was straight after school and was only supposed to take half an hour, her mother had agreed to let her come home by herself on the bus. But by four-thirty it was already getting dark, and the boys pouring out of the school and lining up under the bus shelter were not the ones she knew, from the play. These were a scary-looking lot with shaved, bristly heads, leprous complexions, and army boots several sizes too big for them. They obviously took exception to Francie for being a girl and waiting at their bus stop wearing a posh private school uniform. Because of the cold she had on her green school beret, with her school badge on the front, emblazoned with the motto *Ad Altorium.*

A Latin scholar with a fearsome metal brace on his teeth, to which some of his lunch was still sticking, leaned close to her face to translate.

"To . . . higher . . . things," he announced triumphantly, as though it proved she was the snob they had all taken her to be.

"To hire things!" chanted his more ignorant cronies, a mistake Francie understood all too well, as she'd made it herself as a new girl. She'd assumed that her school must be short on books and equipment, and be proclaiming the virtues of borrowing. But the boys had different ideas.

"For hire then, are you, darling?" they said, closing in on her, jostling her with the sharp corners of their kit bags. "What do you charge then, eh? Bet you're all right under all that. Got green panties on an' all, 'ave you?" One of them offered her fifteen pence and another snatched the beret off her head. He tossed it to his mate, who punched it to make it pot-shaped and did a graphic mime of crapping into it, with awful grunting sound effects. It was very realistic. Toby and Roy would have been proud of him.

"Give that back," said Francie as calmly as she could, but there was no bus in sight and under her pleated tunic her knees were knocking with fright. Through the gloom she thought she saw someone she knew coming out of the school gates, and she waved wildly to attract his attention. Luckily he saw her at once and came hurrying toward her, taller and older and miles more authoritative than any of the boys who had it in for her. And in the sweeping relief of that moment it seemed he must surely be a true friend, rather than her archenemy, Richard.

"Hello, Francie," he said in surprise, and at his just knowing her name, the skinheads turned their backs and moved away. The comic who had hold of her beret let it drop to the ground like a hot potato.

"What are you doing here today?" said Richard. "Has the dreaded Toby called you to a special torture session of your own?"

"I've been having a fitting," said Francie, gazing desperately down the road, but it was necessary to say more, to engage him in conversation until the wretched bus condescended to come. Out of the corner of her eye she could see her beret being edged along the gutter by a black boot. With an effort of will she looked at Richard and smiled. It was not as difficult as she expected.

"My costume's awful," she said. "I don't like it a bit."

"Awful in what way?" he said, leaning back indolently against the edge of the bus shelter. "Describe it to me in gory detail." He looked at her sideways under his spiky eyelashes with amused, calculating eyes. He was obviously keen on storing up bits of information that could later be used against her. It crossed her mind that he might go straight back to Toby and Roy and tell them how vain and ungrateful she was. But just then the brainbox in the brace sidled up again. Picking up her muddy beret, he put it into her hand with a steel smirk.

"I think this must have fallen off your head," he said, and rather than have to say thank you, Francie turned back to Richard.

"That's just it," she said. "My dress hasn't got any details. It's completely plain. It's made of this awful dull gray stuff. It's completely boring."

"Perfect," said Richard, flicking the corners of his mouth in a smug smile.

"What do you mean, perfect?" said Francie furiously. She brushed at the black mud on her beret. She'd have been better off after all being insulted by thugs.

"I mean," said Richard, "that the audience won't be able to take their eyes off you. What could be better? There you'll be in the middle of the stage wearing nothing but the color of your own eyes, and everyone else dolled up to the nines around you. It's a well-known theatrical trick, didn't you know?"

"What is?" said Francie suspiciously.

"Being plain when everyone else is fancy. Coming into a roomful of color dressed in monochrome. It focuses the audience's attention."

"Does it indeed," said Francie with as much sarcasm as she could manage.

"Of course it does. Actors are always getting up to that sort of thing. Talking quietly when everyone else is shouting. Or standing stock-still while everyone else is leaping about. It works like a charm, every time."

Francie could see his little game. He wanted her to come on as Amelia looking like a mouse and mumble her way through her lines with her arms pinned to her sides. That way he could prove once and for all to Toby and Roy how right he had been to advise them against her.

After the long wait, four buses, all with the same number, were converging on the stop. The first one drew up, packed with people, and the boys began pushing and shoving their way aboard.

Richard took hold of Francie's arm.

"Let them go," he said in a quiet voice, as though he'd

been aware all along of the trouble she'd been in. "Wait for the next one." With his free hand he hailed the bus behind. The bus driver, who looked set to sail straight past the stop, did not dare disobey Richard's lordly gesture. Francie was to have an empty bus all to herself.

Still holding her arm, Richard jumped onto the platform with her, and then just as quickly jumped off again as the bus started to move. Despite herself, Francie liked the way he did that. There was something swift and impulsive about his action that delighted her to her bones. She would have liked to have seen him do it again and again, that lithe, unexpected leap on and off, on his long, lazy legs, up and down, now here, now gone, but the bus was already speeding away and he was left loping along in its wake.

"Forget the boyfriend," said the bus conductor, in the presumptuous tone he kept specially for endearing himself to children. "There's no man worth falling off the bus for. Move along inside, please."

Francie did as she was told and sat down. Inside her coat sleeve there was a buzzing feeling in her upper arm where Richard had grabbed her: a slightly sore sense of irritation—his fingers must have left a red mark. The bus went irresponsibly fast with its light load of one, and Francie was elated by the speed. Everything around her seemed unusually loud and bright. The lighted windows of posh and poor Putney raced by in impressionistic flashes of grace and squalor. All the earlier horrors of the afternoon—the dullness of her dress, the mothers with their pins, the boys with her beret—were wiped out by one extraordinary thought: that Rosanna's insinuations might be true after all.

15

It was on the day before the dress rehearsal that Bat died. Francie's father was out seeing a client, and Jessica had gone off for the day with her boyfriend, so Francie and her mother were alone in the house. Its being Saturday morning, Francie was allowed to sleep in, and she was lying blissfully under her duvet when the tone of her mother's voice calling from the kitchen made her leap out of her bed and go tearing down the stairs without her dressing gown and slippers.

There was an enormous puddle in the middle of the kitchen floor. Bat was standing in the middle of it looking dazed and ashamed.

"He's never done that before," said Francie's mother, who was close to tears. "Not even when he first came here from Battersea. *And* he's been coughing up foam. Go and get dressed quickly, Francie. We'll have to get him to the vet."

At the word *vet,* Bat began slinking toward the back door.

"He wants to go out," said Francie, rushing to open the door for him, not caring where she stepped.

"Look where you're going! Now I suppose you'll go and tread wet feet all over the carpet," shouted her mother.

How could she fuss about such things at a time like this?

"Don't shout," said Francie, shouting herself in her panic. "Bat'll think you're cross with *him.*"

But Bat had already taken himself out into the garden in disgrace.

Francie left her mother mopping up the floor and rushed upstairs to get her clothes on. Suddenly, simple things like putting on her jeans and doing up the buttons of her jersey seemed fraught with difficulty.

When she got downstairs again, her mother was on the phone talking to the vet. She could hear her arranging to bring Bat straight over.

Francie got his lead off the hall stand and rushed out into the garden to call him. But he didn't come. He was nowhere to be seen.

She ran back inside the house again and searched upstairs and down, calling his name frantically from room to room.

Her mother called from the hall, "I didn't hear him come in. I think he must still be in the garden. He's probably hiding under a bush or something. That's what they do . . ." Her voice trailed away, leaving the sentence unfinished. But Francie could tell how it went on. That's what they do when they're dying.

She rushed back out into the garden, followed by her mother, and eventually they found him curled up against the fence under a camellia bush. He'd made himself a hole in the earth to lie in, as though to save them the trouble of digging a grave. It was a wet, windy day and he was trembling from head to foot.

"We must get him out of the rain," said Francie's mother.

"Come on, Bat," said Francie coaxingly, but he wouldn't budge.

"Put his lead on, quickly," said her mother. "I told the vet we'd be over straightaway."

Francie hesitated. To her shame she had a sudden fear of touching the dog with his strange bloodshot, wolfish eyes.

"I don't think he can recognize us," she said.

Her mother took the lead impatiently and hooked it to his collar. But still Bat wouldn't get to his feet. All the strength he had left he used to resist.

"It's no use, we'll have to lift him," she said, but he was a big dog, and deep in the shrubbery as he was, it was impossible for Francie and her mother to get a grip on him.

"What are we going to do?" said Francie's mother helplessly. Her voice sounded curiously high and small, and to Francie's alarm she was shaking. Francie had imagined the horror of this day over and over again, but it was her own feelings she'd expected to have to deal with, not other people's.

"Perhaps we ought to just leave him here," she said, "if it's where he wants to be."

"But it's so cold for him," said Francie's mother in the same childlike tone.

"I'll go and get a blanket," said Francie, and she started off toward the house.

"Not one of the best ones!" called her mother in a much more normal voice.

Not one of the best ones! Francie would have grabbed the goosedown duvet off her own bed if she'd thought it would bring Bat any comfort. But the nearest thing to hand was the old army blanket that lined the bottom of his basket.

She rushed back in time to see Bat being led firmly by the collar across the grass toward her. His legs were sliding under him, but he was walking. Francie was relieved to see her mother looking brisk and bossy once more.

"He got up when you went and tried to follow you," she said. "Get the car keys and lock the house. I'll take him straight out to the car."

Getting him up onto the car seat was the hardest part. It was too far from the ground. He wanted to be helpful but he couldn't jump. His legs failed him. With a last huge-hearted effort he let them propel him from behind. Francie sat in the back with him, clutching the smelly blanket around his shoulders. Her mother's driving was for once quite fast and efficient, but as it was a rainy Saturday morning, the main streets of Barnes were swarming with as many cars as people. Bat's breathing was getting very bad. Through his brown and white fur his nose looked blue. "Come on, come *on!*" Francie pleaded with every red light that stood in their way.

When they pulled up across the road from the vet's clinic, Bat had a sudden revival of wits. He knew exactly where they were. Nothing on God's earth was going to get him out of the car.

"We'll have to get help," said Francie's mother. "You stay here with Bat. I'll go and tell the vet we're here."

Bat curled up again like a puppy, in the same stubborn position he had taken up in the bushes. Although he was wide awake, he sounded as though he was snoring. Francie sat beside him with her hand on the back of his neck. There was a terrible trembling in her palm, which might have been hers or his, she couldn't tell.

"Don't," she whispered to him over and over again.

"Don't." She tried to breathe calmly and evenly, as though somehow her breathing would influence his. She tried to tell him with the weight of her hand that everything was all right, although she knew it was a lie: any minute now, things would be getting worse for him. The thing he dreaded was about to happen. Any minute now the vet would come and get him and carry him into the office. He would die rather than go in there.

Suddenly, Francie knew that she and Bat were involved in a race against time, different from the race to get here. She had been praying the wrong prayer. He would die rather than go in there. Oh, if only he could make it in time.

On the other side of the road, Francie's mother and the vet emerged from the office. They stood about on the doorstep, fiddling around with umbrellas, and then started toward the gate. Francie's heart sank.

But as the gate clicked shut, Bat suddenly gave a great whinnying sigh and twisted his face so that the cleverest, most knowing part of him, his black, quivering nostrils, were squashed against the upholstered back of the seat. He seemed to push with all his faint might, and with that push, all the air he had left in his body was squeezed out of him. A great relaxation came over him, and all the struggle and strain going on under Francie's hand seemed to ebb away through her fingers. With that sigh, with that turn of his face to the wall, it seemed to her that he gave up the ghost. It was not an expression she'd understood or even thought about before, but somehow when those words came unexpectedly into her mind, they stuck there. Looking back on this day, as she did for years, she knew that that was exactly what Bat had done. He had given up the ghost. And somehow it made her proud of him. Dying was something he had done, not something that had happened to him.

She was still sitting there with her hand on the dead dog's neck when the car door opened. Her mother's distress was suddenly not for Bat at all but for her white, blank-faced daughter.

"I'm so sorry, darling," she kept saying. "I should never have left you alone with him. If I'd known it would all be over so quickly . . ."

The vet checked the dog's eyes and pulse and then covered him with the blanket and carried him with Francie's mother's help into the clinic. Francie stayed where she was. She had no desire to know where the body was going or what would become of it. There was a tiny trace of blood on the upholstery of the seat beside her that had come out of Bat's mouth. If her mother so much as mentioned it, she knew she would scream.

But when her mother came back to the car, she didn't notice anything, she didn't even seem to know which way the car was facing, let alone how to get home.

"I'm so sorry I left you," she said again, driving vaguely toward Richmond. "If only your father or Jessica had been there. You're the last one who should have had to cope with that."

"I'd rather it be me than them," said Francie. "I wouldn't want to come home and find Bat just not there."

"No," said her mother, "I don't suppose I would either."

After a while she turned up a side road and stopped the car so she could look up where they were in the street finder and have a chance to cry.

Francie leaned over from the backseat and put her arms around her mother's neck, but she didn't cry herself. She didn't want to think about how she felt just yet. If she started crying now, how on earth would she stop in time for tomorrow's rehearsal?

16

The first time Francie saw Richard in his costume for the Earl of Cardigan, she had what Rosanna would have described as a womb-wave. Personally, she would simply have called it an attack of nerves at the prospect of the dress rehearsal: butterflies in the stomach, which happened to coincide with Richard's walking past her in the corridor, brilliantly arrayed in his tight red trousers, long boots, blue, gold-braided jacket, and high plumed hat. The costume department had certainly done *him* proud.

He had gone in for a lot of extravagant facial whiskers, and under his bristling gold moustachios it was more difficult than ever to tell whether that sardonic curl of his lip actually constituted a smile. Francie didn't wait to find out. She darted into the girls' dressing room before he could make any patronizing remarks about the glorious simplicity of her plain gray dress. In the light of his own dazzling appearance, a compliment from him might very well make her throw up.

The dressing room was actually a classroom that happened to be close to the stage. The dressing and making up had to be done in the aisles between the desks. On the blackboard the boys had chalked up messages for the girls: a rude French word, *merde,* and "Break a leg." Apparently, in theater, it was good luck to wish people bad luck.

Francie had been wandering around for quite some time with her hair loose, waiting to have it put up in a Victorian style. But the person who was supposed to be doing it never seemed to be free, and when Francie borrowed a few hairpins from the tray and tried to have a go at it herself, the beastly woman snapped at her and told her to wait her turn.

"I've had specific instructions about your hair," she said pompously, pointing with one of her sticks of makeup to the drawing Francie had been shown at her fitting. "Kindly just leave it to me."

Francie put the pins back and waited. The most important thing to do was to stay calm. Somehow or other today had to be got through. Her hair was the least of her problems. The silly old cow could be as nasty as she liked: it was sympathy Francie dreaded. As long as nobody knew about Bat, she would be all right. Proper actors had to cope with dreadful things happening all the time. They had to appear onstage laughing and singing even if their wives were in hospital or their houses were burning down. The show must go on, and all that.

But this show would be going on without her if her hair wasn't started in a minute. Overture and beginners had been called and everyone except Francie and Emily, who weren't in the Brighton scene, had gone up onto the stage. The band was already striking up with the opening number and the hairdressing woman was still fiddling around with Emily's makeup for the Miller's Wife, trying to make her look middle-aged.

"Emily doesn't come on until two scenes after me," said Francie in a small voice, but still the woman took no notice. Francie thought Emily might say something on her behalf, but at that moment she was having peevish-looking lines painted at the corners of her mouth, which perhaps made it awkward for her to speak.

Francie gave a loud sigh and cleared her throat. The makeup woman glared at her over Emily's shoulder. She had hairpins in her mouth and spoke through clenched teeth.

"How many times do I have to tell you to be patient?" she said. "I'll get to you in a minute."

From the stage Francie could hear the rhythmic stamp of the boys' feet marching about the stage.

> "We're Cardigan's boys,
> We're his favorite toys,
> He drills us from morning till night,"

they sang, and her heart began to thud in time to the music:

> "He parades us, upbraids us
> And often degrades us,
> But we're never expected to fight."

Francie took a deep breath.

"My first entrance is in the scene after next," she said. "If my hair isn't done soon, I'll have to go on looking like this."

"You really are an extremely rude little girl," said the woman, spitting pins. She penciled in one final furrow on poor Emily, who escaped her clutches at last, looking more like the miller's terminally ill grandmother than his bonny, bouncing wife.

Richard could be heard alone on the stage now, half singing, half speaking his first number: "An Officer Must Always Be a Gentleman." Something in his clipped, haughty accents infected Francie with an unexpected grandeur of her own. She swept up a fistful of hairpins and thrust them forcibly into the Old Cow's hand.

"I'll be having a word about you later," said the OC furiously, "with the Powers that Be."

"Say what you like," said Francie in a loud, actressy voice: "Just do my hair, *now.*"

Where good manners had failed, temperament worked like a charm. The woman blinked, twice, and did as she was told. Badly, of course. And piercing Francie's scalp with the pins. But she hurried as fast as she could. There was no hope now of getting Francie's hair to remotely resemble the style pictured in the design, but she did manage to push it up into some semblance of a bun. Francie could hear the two captains Reynolds launching into their duet "He Can't Tell the One from the Other." Ready or not, she wrenched herself from the pin-woman's grasp.

"Come back here, I haven't finished," the woman shouted, but Francie was gone, pins flying from her as she raced along the corridor toward the wings. Her entrance was from the other side of the stage. She had to wriggle her way across in the narrow space behind the canvas backdrop, causing violent ripples across the genteel Victorian street.

Joe was already onstage, introducing Lord Cardigan to his nonexistent wife. Francie stumbled and nearly fell over the scenery as she rushed to take his arm. She was without her props: her parasol and shawl were on the table in the wings behind her. She thought she would faint with fright.

"Ah, but I remember your wife's beauty all too well,"

said Richard, raising his eyebrows at Francie's ungloved hand as he lifted it to his lips.

"Indeed, sir, we have met before," she managed to say, although her voice came out much higher than usual.

"Where in bloody hell were you?" hissed Joe as they paraded decorously on past the elegant London town houses.

Francie rolled her eyes comically upward to indicate the arrangement on top of her head.

"Where in bloody hell do you think?" she answered without moving her lips; and swearing made her brave, she could see why theatricals went in for it. You needed nerve and gall to sashay about like this in the cruel glare of the lights, pretending to be someone you weren't. Joe looked at her with new interest, and from that moment on the play seemed to sweep her up and carry her along like a wave. She hated all the little hitches and hiccups that happened because it was a dress rehearsal: every time the scenery got stuck or the lighting failed, or the band got out of tempo with itself, she stood about tapping her foot, dying to get back into character. Even when in the middle of "Just for Me," she tossed her head and a coil of her hair flopped down onto her shoulder to a loud giggle from the wings, she didn't blush, or fluff her lines. She simply incorporated her tumbling locks into the passion of the song. Frankly, she felt safer on the stage than she did off. She was relieved for a while to be a woman in a gray dress with all-absorbing problems of her own. For all Amelia's difficulties with men and their wicked ways, at least for the duration of the play Francie didn't have to be a child whose dog had died yesterday, who could be bossed around by amateur hairdressers just because they were grown up.

When the play was over, Toby called the cast down into the auditorium for notes. Notes meant telling everyone how dreadful they were when it was too late for them to do anything about it. Constantly pushing his hair out of his eyes before it had time to fall back in, Toby tore the performance apart. They were too soft, too loud, out of tune, out of time. The windmill scene was a mess: he had hardly been able to see the duel for spectators, who were blocking the sight lines. There was too much "mugging" (face-making) going on at the police station—people were trying to be funny and spoiling the jokes. The courtroom scene was flabby, needed cutting, and what had happened to the Peers? For some reason they had all developed cockney accents. As for the final street scene . . . he shuddered to think how much work needed to be done before they opened on Wednesday.

"Some of us," he said, eyeing Francie, "don't even seem to have mastered the art of getting onto the stage on cue."

Then Roy, soaked with sweat from his struggles with the band, set about organizing the curtain calls. In the light of Toby's comments it was hard to imagine the audience bothering to clap at all. But Roy was optimistic. He went so far as to arrange some encores. There was to be a reprise of Harvey and Amelia's song, "We Shall Live Our Lives Together," and then the whole cast would sing "It's a Matter of Honor" as they took their final bows.

Just as everyone was beginning to warm to the idea of being cheered and showered with rose petals, Toby brought them down to size again, this time by plowing into the principals. One by one, in front of the whole cast, he listed their individual faults in detail. Francie didn't mind. Considering how sarcastic he could be, she counted herself lucky to have got off so lightly over the business of being late. His comments about her performance seemed perfectly fair and constructive.

"You're much too meek at the beginning," he told her. "I thought for a moment you really were going to succumb to Cardigan's advances. Keep that submissive quality for the scenes at home with Joe. He is your husband, after all. Lean back in his arms when you sing. We really need to feel that you trust him."

Francie nodded and got up to go with the rest of the cast, who were beginning to drift away. She felt cheerful and relieved that today's ordeal was over.

"Oh, and by the way, Frances," Toby called after her. "Do something about your hair before Wednesday night, will you? It looks like a dog's dinner."

It was as though he had turned on a tap. Tears were suddenly pouring down Francie's face. It was strange—she didn't really feel upset, just embarrassed to have all this water she couldn't control spurting out of her eyes.

"What's the matter?" people said, coming up to her in concern, but before anyone could touch her, she rushed from the auditorium and down the long corridor. Luckily the staff lavatory was unlocked, so she took herself in there, where the plumbing could cope, if she couldn't. This was what she'd been afraid of. Once she started crying, she wouldn't be able to stop. She turned on the taps to drown out the noise she was making and leaned over the basin, trying to cry herself out. Deliberately she let the image of Bat break through the blank wall she had constructed inside her head.

And strangely, when he burst in on her memory, he wasn't old anymore, but full of youthful energy, bounding toward her as through a field of high grass, higher than he was, so that sometimes he would completely disappear: one second the field would be completely empty and dogless, and the next the grass would part and his beautiful brown ears would flap into view. As fast as he was traveling, he never really got any nearer. But her mind's eye got stronger and just as she could picture him in detail, she felt a hand on her shoulder.

It was Joe. He leaned forward over her and turned off the taps.

"Toby can be a real bastard," he said sympathetically, "but you shouldn't let him get to you like that."

"He's not . . ." hiccuped Francie. "I'm not . . . It's not . . ."

"Not what?" said Joe patiently.

"You're not . . . supposed to be in here," said Francie, and it was true: the staff lavatory was for female teachers and girls.

"So what?" said Joe, and led her to a small bench under the towel dispenser, where he sat her down beside him. It was quite a squash for two.

"I don't know why you're so upset," he said. "He said much worse things to me."

Francie reached up above her head for a paper towel.

"It's not . . . Toby," she said. "It's nothing to do with the play."

"Isn't it?" said Joe, suddenly twice as interested.

Francie blew her nose.

"I don't really want to talk about it," she said, and they sat for a moment, side by side, while the last of Francie's convulsive sobs subsided. She didn't really mind him there. She was used to having him beside her on the stage. After a while he guided her head sideways until it rested on his chest. "You'll feel better if you tell me," he said.

Perhaps she would. As her husband in the play, he seemed to have a right to know. Lean back, Toby had said, we need to feel you trust him.

"I don't want anyone else to find out," said Francie. "Promise you won't spread it around if I tell you."

Joe hugged her closer. "What do you think I am?" he said.

So Francie told him. "My dog died," she said.

"Oh," said Joe in a disappointed voice, but he was right,

she did feel better, and she began to tell him everything, about the trip to the vet and being left alone with Bat when it actually happened. Her face was buried in his shirt now: he didn't seem to mind her mascara getting all over his frilled white front.

"There you are, you see," he said. "You did need to talk about it. You should have told Toby and he would have told the cast. Everyone would have been really sympathetic."

"Oh, no!" said Francie in horror. "I'd have died if they'd known. They might have remembered."

"Remembered what?"

"That I *acted* being my dog in improvisation. I pretended to *be* him when he was old and ill, for a *game.*"

She raised her blotchy face to look at him so that he could see the shame she felt at what she had done. And suddenly, rapidly, from what seemed like another scene altogether, his blue eyes came so close, they went out of focus: lowering his face, he covered her unsuspecting lips with his open mouth.

It was not the kiss that shocked and disgusted Francie. It was the timing of it, the moment that he chose. She didn't know much about sex, but she knew that this was not a sexual moment. There was a bit in the play when he had to kiss her on the cheek and that didn't embarrass her at all. In fact, she rather looked forward to it: she liked his chewing-gum breath and the suctiony feeling of his lips. But to trap her now, like this, in her distress, probing at her grief with that wet, slippery tongue, was worse than stealing from her. It was as though he were laughing in her face.

He was strong, and held her down, so it took all the strength she had to push him away. He fell off the bench onto the floor, where he sat for a moment, looking rather foolish and surprised. He was obviously not used to being spurned. Rosanna's words came back to Francie: "He's always around the back of the lavatories getting off with anything in a skirt he can lay his hands on." Even the setting was right.

Joe got up, brushing at the tight black trousers of his costume.

"Well," he said, "you certainly are a proper little prick-tease, aren't you? Don't try and tell me you weren't asking for it."

Francie could see exactly the sort of boy he was now. If you let him kiss you, you were a slag. If you didn't, you were frigid.

"I just wasn't in the mood," she said stiffly. "You ought to've been able to tell."

"Yes," he said, walking nonchalantly to the door, "I should, shouldn't I." He timed his exit line perfectly. "I should have been able to tell from the way you were blubbing, what a baby you were."

One thing he had done for her anyway, Francie thought as she took a look at her bloodshot eyes in the mirror: he had thoroughly dried up her tears. Her lips were still red and puffed up from crying. It gave them a pouting, suggestive look, like evidence—would people be able to tell she'd been kissing? In the circumstances, she didn't think Joe would want to show off about it. He had better ways of getting back at her than that. She lingered in the washroom, unhooking the back of her dress and taking down what was left of her hairstyle. She might as well give him time to do his worst.

And sure enough, as she approached the girls' dressing room their voices floated out to her.

"You know *why* Francie was in such a state, don't you."

"Yes, what *was* the matter with her? Rushing off like that in tears. You'd think at least she'd been raped."

"Actually, her dog died. Apparently she blurted it all out to Joe."

"Poor Francie. She really loved her dog. She was always going on about him. You know, the old cocker spaniel."

There was a scuffle, a silence, and then giggles. No doubt some bright spark was down on the floor, pretending to be Francie pretending to be Bat. Francie was too tired to care anymore what they did. She only wanted to avoid the embarrassment of catching them at it. She waited patiently outside the door for them to change the subject. Her one desire was to get out of her costume and go home. She had definitely made up her mind not to be an actress. She was giving up the theater for good.

"Hey, Francie, I'm glad I caught you."

It was Richard, coming down the corridor toward her. Francie sighed. With her blotchy face, he was all she needed. Not that she cared a toss what he thought of her. She was giving up men as well.

In his jeans, without his moustache, he looked, unexpectedly, rather young.

"You all right?" he said. "You look a bit rumpled. Have you been having a punch-up with the wardrobe department? They got quite a lot of flak, you know, for making you late."

"Did they?" said Francie in surprise. "They'll hate me even more now, I suppose, on Wednesday."

"If I were you," said Richard, lowering his voice, "I wouldn't let the old bats in this place"—he had said "old Bats," but Francie didn't flinch— "get their hands on you. There must be someone at home who could do your hair. Arrive with it already done."

Could she trust him? Or was he just trying to get her into more trouble? If recent events were anything to go by, she was the last person capable of telling a friend from an enemy.

"I'll think about it," she said cautiously. "I certainly don't want to go through another experience like this."

"You were really good today, by the way," said Richard in an offhand voice that made the words sound as though they meant the opposite. "Bloody good, actually, in case nobody bothered to mention it to you."

"So were you," admitted Francie, although she doubted if a person of his obvious confidence and talent needed any compliments from her.

Apparently he did. He seemed absurdly gratified. "Did you think so?" he said anxiously. "I thought I messed up the seduction scene badly. I made you seem meek by being too bullying. If he's such a womanizer, I think his technique would be subtler than that. I think he'd come on all gentle and gallant with her to start with. Then when her defenses were down he could suddenly move in on her. That way it'd seem more sadistic."

Francie heartily agreed.

"What if when you made a pass at me, I pushed you?" she said, suddenly feeling rather excited, despite her new indifference to the acting profession. "I mean really hard, so you fell over. You could say your line 'You'll pay for this!' from down on the ground. I mean with all the women you're supposed to have seduced, you wouldn't really *mind* about Amelia. You'd just hate to be made to look a fool."

"Yes," said Richard eagerly, "why didn't we think of that before?" and they tried it out right there, where they were.

"Jesus," said Richard, reeling halfway down the corridor from her shove, "I don't think Toby'll be calling you meek again in a hurry!"

Back in the dressing room, Francie felt surprisingly cheered up. For some complicated reason that she couldn't be bothered to work out, pushing Richard had made her feel better about Bat. She no longer dreaded anyone mentioning the word dog. She quite looked forward to a bit of sympathy now.

But nobody glanced up as she came in. The girls carried on chatting to each other about how knackered they were and exactly what they fancied to eat. They seemed a bit scared of Francie, as people often are of the bereaved.

With everyone avoiding looking at her, she ran very little risk of being seen. The real risk lay in trusting Richard's advice.

The drawing of Amelia's hairstyle was still spread out on the desk beside the makeup tray. Francie fingered the corner of it doubtfully. Then with a shrug she rolled it up and stuffed it into her bag.

17

"What's this?" said Francie's father scornfully. "The nose is completely out of drawing."

"The face doesn't matter," said Francie impatiently. "It's the hair we have to copy."

"That's not a typical 1840s style," said her mother, getting a book of old fashion plates down off the shelf. "Look, you should have ringlets, like this, over your ears. Or your hair in long twists on your neck, wired with rosebuds and ribbons."

"It's got to be *plain,*" said Francie, beginning to get in a panic. "It's got to look like the *picture.*"

"Leave her alone," said Jessica. "I'll do your hair for you, darling."

Considering they'd been dead against the play in the first place, it was amazing how Francie's parents fussed over her when it came to the opening night. Her mother made her a special early meal of filet steak and spinach as soon as she got home from school.

"You must have at least two hours to digest it," she said. "The rest of us can get a hamburger or something in Wandsworth, after we've dropped you off."

Her father had bought her some flowers: pink roses wrapped in cellophane. *Good luck to my darling Francie,* said the card, in his meticulous illustrator's hand.

Even Jessica managed to subdue her ego for the evening: she kept out of rows and out of the bathroom and was standing ready to go by the front door when the time came to leave, having changed her outfit only three times.

Francie's hair was a joint effort between Jessica and her mother. They decided to dispense with the bun altogether, so that the parting ran right down the back of her head, but the coils over her ears were faithful to the design, and looked quite soft and flattering, though in fact they were tight and rock hard: no amount of head tossing would budge them. Jessica did her makeup for her as well, subtly, so that her features looked larger but not painted.

"You look lovely," she said when she'd finished, and squirted the bare back of Francie's neck with a shower of her best bluebell scent.

Francie felt carsick on the way, even though she'd been made to sit importantly in the front. The traffic was dreadful and the car fumes made things worse, but she didn't really mind if they were late. In a way she was dreading the time before the play started more than the performance itself. She imagined being chased between the desks and up and down the corridors of Dubbs by irate women wielding hairbrushes. She must keep out of their way, but how? She certainly wasn't going to take refuge in the ladies' lavatory again.

But "backstage" (for that was the only way to describe the brightly lit schoolrooms tonight), it was easy to be lost in the bustle. In her room everyone was barging about, knocking into chair legs with their crinolines, trying out their top notes as they went.

"Hello!" they cried, wildly excited to see her, and she was excited to see them, even though they'd met each other a few hours ago at school. It was like arriving at a party: everyone was friendly and flushed and witty as though they'd been drinking champagne. Certainly a sniffer could have got quite high by just breathing: the air was full of the concentrated smell of cheap hairspray and spirit gum.

There were more mothers than usual helping with makeup and hair and all of them were near nervous breakdown: they were only too relieved to clap eyes on a girl who'd already been dealt with. Francie let each one think another mother had done her hair, which was true, another mother *had*. She walked backward quite a lot, in case her bunless profile caused a scene, but nobody said a word, except "For goodness' sake look where you're going!"

To her delight she discovered that her gray dress had been slightly altered. The neckline had been lowered and widened, and a white lace collar had been sewn on. She got changed at once, even though it was miles too early. After her experience at the dress rehearsal, she wanted the business of her appearance finished and out of the way. She needed time to think.

She didn't get it, of course. There were too many people bursting in with messages of leg-fracturing good luck. Much play was made on the words of the title *An Affair of Honor.* Rosanna had an anonymous card that said: *Never mind about the honor, how about an affair,* and there was excited speculation as to who had sent it. The girls were rushing around asking selected boys for their autographs, in order to get samples of their handwriting. A telegram was read out from Sir Henry Dubbs's grandson's widow, congratulating them all warmly on the performances they hadn't yet given. Roy came in, full of good cheer despite the appalling fit of his conductor's tails, and told them to relax and enjoy themselves.

"Give it all you've got—show them what you're made of," he said, perhaps to reassure himself since so much of what *he* was made of was bulging out over the tight waist of his dress trousers. Even Toby had a last-minute go at telling them they were wonderful, on the off chance that encouragement might succeed where sarcasm had failed. Everyone seemed to believe him although they were quite aware of the games he played: didn't they remember "We Are the Way We Are Treated"?

"You're going to be great," he said to Francie, patting her head where her bun should have been.

Francie nearly fell over. She could hardly stay on her feet, let alone remember her first line. On top of her nerves, she had problems with her personal relationships.

Playing Amelia had been easy enough when she'd liked Joe and hated Richard. Everything she had to say and do had been a natural extension of her true feelings. But now she had to act against the grain. Despising Joe as she now did, she was still expected to look at him with love brimming in her eyes. And Richard, whom she'd loathed from the bottom of her heart, could no longer carry conviction for her as a real-life villain. How could she have got into such an appalling muddle? She kept clear of them both in the wings, and closed her eyes tightly, trying to psych herself back into her original innocent state of blind prejudice. She tried to re-create that first day of rehearsal, when Joe had been so nice and Richard so completely insufferable. But as soon as she opened her eyes the facts came straight back: the thought of Joe's slippery kiss still made her shudder. Supposing she shuddered like that when he kissed her onstage? What if the audience could tell, as Rosanna could, all along, that she had a secret crush on Richard? Watching him now as he harangued his troops in tones of revolting pomposity, she realized it was true. He was gorgeous.

She wished she could believe she was dazzled by his costume: the flashes of gold on his royal-blue jacket, the magnificence of his whiskers. But in fact his uniform and soldierly bearing disguised the things she liked most about him—his languid, loose-limbed walk, his flicking, dipping mouth and sidelong glances. She'd even come to admire his sandy complexion, reddened now in hideous, blustering wrath. Apart from anything else, he was a bloody good actor. To look at him now you'd never believe he could be sweet. And sweet was what he'd been to her lately. There was no other word for it. *He tried to stop me getting the part,* she reminded herself. But even that didn't seem much of a crime to a person waiting in the wings on a first night, petrified at the prospect of going on. Nevertheless, the evidence damned him and she clung to it fiercely, as though it were the only thing that stood between her and certain failure. "He tried to stop me getting the part," she was still muttering over and over to herself as Joe took up his position at her side, ready for their entrance in the street scene.

Was he still sulking? It was too late to find out. Characters from the scene before were tumbling into the wings, as though they took the break-a-leg motto literally. The audience was clapping enthusiastically. Things were obviously going well. *So far,* thought Francie fatalistically as Joe took her arm and swept her onto the stage.

No sooner had she hit the streets of Victorian England than Francie made a strange discovery. Where Joe and Richard were concerned, there was no problem. All those long, hard weeks of rehearsal yielded up their blessing: she knew the boys better as characters than she did as people. Amelia's hatred of Lord Cardigan had a life of its own. When his lips brushed her gloved hand, she shuddered automatically. Recent developments in Francie's feelings didn't come into it. How could they affect Amelia, whom the earl had tried to ruin? And her attitude to her husband, Harvey Tuckett, was equally untouched. The constancy of her love for him blotted out all Francie's personal experiences with Joe. She could look into his blue eyes with absolute innocence and trust. And it was clearly the same for him. In his dealings with Amelia there were no overtones at all of Francie's having pushed him to the floor. He was the same old Harvey Tuckett he always had been—kind and brave and true. It was extraordinary, but it was also quite simple. It was because they had done it hundreds of times before.

The audience was another matter. Francie didn't care at *all* for all those people sitting out there in the dark. She kept getting hair-raising glimpses of faces that she knew: her headmistress in the front row; Jessica sitting next to, of all people, Isabel Archer. But after a while the faces sort of joined up and became one person. A crouching, unpredictable, dangerous sort of person, it was true. But someone who from time to time would suddenly do something unexpectedly delightful. Like laugh.

Whenever the audience laughed, the sound ran through the whole cast like a charge of electricity. Everybody wanted to be the one who could make it happen. Boys in quite serious parts started to ad lib a few jokes of their own in order to raise one of those wonderful spontaneous roars. But the audience was not to be controlled. It laughed when it felt like it. Sometimes when the actors were least expecting it to. What tickled it most was when things went slightly wrong. Anyone whose helmet fell off was immediately the star of the show. That was all right if you happened to be playing a funny policeman, but it wasn't the sort of reaction Francie was hoping for as Amelia. The success of her part could only be measured by silence. When it came to her scenes, she was aware of having to calm this audience-person down, keep it still, stop it coughing, make it listen. It was such an absorbingly difficult thing to do that when at the end of the first act, her husband was carried off, wounded, and she was left on the stage for the reprise of "Just for Me," all alone, without anyone to prop her up, she didn't really have time to think about shaking, or losing her voice, or toppling into the orchestra pit. It took all the concentration that her brain and body could muster to draw that restless creature out there in the dark into the spirit of her song.

There was hardly any light on the stage, but what there was fell full on her face. She'd practiced the number moving around a bit, with actions, but the more she just stood there, the less she felt she needed to do. Stand stock-still, Richard had said. She didn't try to project the song out at the audience, as Toby had so often yelled at her to do, but sang it as though to herself, drawing her shawl tightly around her and sometimes even daring to close her eyes. She wanted to make the audience lean forward. She wanted to have enough power to sing softly so that the audience would hold its breath in order to hear.

When the clapping came at the end, the sudden loud noise of it made her jump. She should have been gratified by the applause, but she wasn't, she hated it, for a moment it sort of offended her, breaking in like that, so rudely, on her privacy. Because this was a modern production there was nothing so unthinkable as a curtain to lower, so she just had to stand there, waiting for the blackout, while the audience turned back into separate people, banging their hundreds of pairs of hands together, and she turned back into Francie, who wriggled and blushed and didn't know what to do.

"Bow!" Roy was mouthing from the pit, but just as she got around to it the boys in the lighting box pressed the right button at last and she was able to slink away under cover of darkness, leaving the audience blindly applauding the place where she'd stood.

In the second half of the show, Francie had an extremely busy time. As she wasn't on as Amelia until later in the act, she had to throw a few rags on over the top of her posh gray dress and pass herself off as one of the People of Putney in order to fill out the crowd. She did her best to disguise herself, wrapping her head in a bit of old blanket and blacking out a couple of teeth. But she was sure that the audience couldn't be so stupid as not to recognize her, and was afraid that to anyone who did, her abrupt disintegration into a toothless old crone might seem like some obscure development of the plot. Nevertheless she wanted to pull her weight for the sake of the show, so she danced around the burning effigy of Lord Cardigan with gusto, hurling stones and cockney insults at his window, while on a raised platform representing the inside of the house, Richard and Rosanna (for some reason wearing her bonnet indoors) sang "Noblesse Oblige," a witty song about the tribulations of being born into the aristocracy.

Then it was off with the rags and the tooth enamel and back to the Tuckett household, for the scene where Harvey tells Amelia that if the Lords find Cardigan guilty of dueling, he himself will be sent to prison. "We shall live our lives together," sang Francie and Joe, although their prospect of doing so seemed pretty remote in the circumstances.

Francie was let off being a Member of the Public at the Trial scene, as there was no time for a quick change afterward, and she had to be ready for her last triumphal entry with Joe at the end. The details of the trial, although historically accurate, always struck Francie as dramatically feeble. Of course, the play had to be wound up somehow, but it was just not good enough, she thought, that the Peers should get Cardigan off on a legal quibble simply in order that Harvey and Amelia should be able to sing "We Shall Live Our Lives Together" one more time without fear of arrest. How could they have been so careless as to let the dreadful earl loose to go on in history to lead hundreds of soldiers to their doom?

Such ironies of fate were lost on the audience tonight. The mums and dads had come to see their sons. The real climax of the evening was the Dance of the Dotty Peers. If the boys wanted to be funny, this was their chance and they grabbed it. There were knock-kneed Peers, bandy-legged Peers, Peers who stuttered, Peers who wheezed: the afflictions and eccentricities of the ruling class reached a crescendo as the boys jigged about the stage, their long white wigs (hand-knitted by the mothers) bouncing on their shoulders and falling over their eyes. "The privilege is ours," they sang, and the two smallest Peers grabbed tall Richard by the elbows and tried to make him join in unrehearsed with their dance, which he did, with rather more good nature than was consistent with his character, but who cared? Hurray for a happy ending! Three cheers for Captain Tuckett!

The audience applauded rapturously as Harvey and Amelia were carried downstage on the shoulders of the crowd for the finale. This time Francie was thrilled with the reception. She wanted it to go on and on.

They were given four encores. Holding hands with Joe on one side and Richard on the other, Francie had never felt such comradeship as with the thirty members of this cast who had worked so hard to make this evening happen. Toby and Roy had been right, she thought, with their tireless harping on about the Group. This was what it was all about: holding hands and joining voices and raising the roof together.

The feeling of communion outlasted the curtain calls: in the wings, in the corridor, and in the dressing rooms, the cast all hugged each other violently, as though welcoming one another home after a long and hazardous journey. Francie didn't mind who she threw her arms around— Joe, Richard, spotty Zach, fat Simon: any actor would do.

The audience started coming backstage and telling them how fabulous they'd been. Nobody had a word against them. Francie had lots of fans: particularly her own family. They thought without doubt that she was the best thing in the show, but that was what they *would* think, wouldn't they.

"Rosanna was marvelous, wasn't she?" said Francie, frowning at them anxiously, trying to teach them how to behave in public. "The Peers were great, didn't you think? What did you think of the play as a *whole*?"

Amanda and Sarah from school had come out of loyalty to Francie. "You were really good," they said, with an amazement that had to be genuine. They seemed fonder of her tonight than they had been for quite some time. There was something about having been on the stage that made people want to touch you. Even her headmistress, not known for her demonstrative nature, patted Francie heartily on the back and actually remembered her name.

Isabel Archer came around, with her godfather from the BBC, and kissed Francie on the cheek.

"You really impressed me," she said warmly, really impressing Francie with the generosity of her attitude. Francie was sure she could never have behaved so well herself, in the circumstances.

Compliments from her family and friends were one thing, but when Toby came up to her, Francie's heart was in her mouth.

"You didn't do what I told you to in your song," he said severely, and then he smiled. "You did something much better, you made me cry. And I wasn't the only one. I was standing at the back of the stalls and I saw several grown men snuffling into their handkerchiefs."

"Colds, probably," said Francie, but she liked the idea of reducing other people's fathers to sodden wrecks. She was even more anxious to know if Roy was pleased with her, since it was he who had written the song. But he just gave Francie one of his giant bear hugs, nearly asphyxiating her with the fumes from his sweat-drenched coat.

"That's my girl" was all he gently said.

The girls had to clean the messages off the blackboard and straighten up the desks before they left. There would be lessons in this dressing room first thing in the morning.

"See you tomorrow," the actors called out to each other as they parted. Of all the lovely things Francie had heard that evening, those three words, see you tomorrow, were the best.

18

Thursday, Friday, Saturday—the run of the play flew by like a train roaring through the dark. Francie was aboard, racketing along, experiencing every pitch and lurch of the same long and exhausting journey, night after night. And yet at the same time, part of her seemed to be standing back, a nonpassenger, disorientated by the speed and noise of the carriages as they flashed mysteriously by.

Of course, she could see that it all had to come to an end. There was a limit to how many times you could fill a theater with an audience made up entirely of parents and friends. Late pass, or no late pass, you couldn't go on rolling up to school an hour and a half after everyone else, black-eyed from last night's makeup and knackered out of your wits. In lessons during the day she was just marking time until the evening. At lunchtime, she wandered around in a trance, making little humming noises to herself, to see if she still had a voice. The girls in the play were let off doing their homework, but she knew she would pay for it in the end. The work the class had done without her would have to be made up. Impressed as her parents had been by the production, their patience was wearing thin. After the first night Toby wanted the cast in earlier at five-thirty, for notes and warming up. Francie's mother hit the roof. "You're a *school*girl," she shouted frantically. "When on earth does he expect you to *eat*?"

"Everyone else seems to manage," said Francie, trying to stay calm and polite, since she depended on her mother for lifts.

"I'll be glad when this dreadful play is over," said her mother. "They seem to think they own you, body and soul."

Some things in the show improved with repetition. Others were never quite the same again. The second night, Thursday, felt a bit flat after the excitement and hysteria of the first night, but Toby told them they were better—much more disciplined and relaxed—and he was probably right. Friday was the best performance as far as Francie was concerned: she felt she was just beginning to get the hang of things at last. And then it was Saturday, and suddenly there were no more chances.

The emotional temperature was too high on the last night for the actors to be at their best. The boys got reckless and cheeky and played terrifying practical jokes. Anyone having to read anything out on stage was in dire jeopardy from the jokers, who substituted filthy messages wherever they could. Simon the police inspector, opening a summons at the police station, went purple in the face, spluttered, and couldn't speak again for the rest of the scene. When Francie put up her parasol, a condom fell out and fluttered to the ground at her feet. Not realizing at first what it was, she bent down to pick it up, but before the audience could see what was happening, Richard gave it a kick and it shot into the orchestra pit, where to judge from the wood-notes wild, it must have landed in the wind section. Luckily, Francie was just on her way offstage, so she was able to make it into the wings before she burst into a fit of uncontrollable laughter. Bursting into a fit of uncontrollable laughter *on* the stage was called "corpsing," and it was a good description: if it happened to you, you felt as though you were dying. And, of course, if Toby and Roy caught you, you might as well be dead.

But tonight there were no recriminations. Better a cast trying not to laugh than a cast trying not to cry. Perhaps Toby and Roy had planted the jokes themselves to distract everyone from the miserable fact that it was *all over.*

No one kissed and cuddled as they had on the first night. Everyone just trooped silently off the stage and back to their dressing rooms, as though their reason for being friendly or just knowing each other had suddenly disappeared.

This was exactly the moment that Toby had been waiting for.

"I've got something to tell you," he said, gathering them all around him in the corridor. "I hope you won't all forget your parts overnight, because the BBC are planning to film the show for television as part of a documentary on children's theater. We're probably talking about the middle of July, so don't dash off on holiday early, will you."

A cheer went up, and Roy hastened to explain that the details hadn't been finalized yet and that the show would have to be adapted a bit for television. There would be certain cuts and changes . . .

But nothing he could say could dampen their spirits now. Francie was over the moon. Going back to a normal school life on Monday seemed suddenly a possible alternative to suicide. She couldn't help noticing that Richard was watching her reaction intently. Cool and pale as his eyes were, they burned her face.

"Exciting, isn't it," she said as she passed him, but he wasn't smiling.

"Coming to the party?" he said rather gruffly.

"I don't think so," said Francie, meaning I don't think I'll be allowed to. "I didn't know there was one."

"It's at Jed's," said Richard. "Everyone's invited."

"I'll have to see," said Francie, meaning I'll have to see if my father will let me.

He wouldn't, of course.

"It's nearly eleven o'clock already," he said. "When's it going to be over, three o'clock in the morning? Do you honestly expect your mother or me to turn out at that hour to fetch you?"

"Most people are staying the night, I expect," said Francie, but she knew he wouldn't stand for it.

"Most people are boys and older than thirteen," he said, predictably enough.

Across the aisle, Rosanna was having the same argument with *her* father, who had at last turned up to see the play. Only she wasn't wasting time listening to reason.

"I've *got* to go!" she shouted, bursting out into loud and embarrassing sobs.

Susceptible to emotional blackmail, her father was caving in fast. A minute or two later it was all arranged. He would pick up both Rosanna and Francie any time up to two a.m. —they could ring him if they needed him earlier: he was entirely at their beck and call. Rosanna was staying the night at his flat in Chelsea, but it wouldn't be much of a detour to drop Francie home to Barnes on the way back. Francie's father offered to take the girls *to* the party, but no, Rosanna's father was only too glad to do that as well. Apparently he was prepared to drive halfway across London day or night to get his daughter's hysteria off his conscience.

Francie's father was forced to give in gracefully.

"Are you sure you've got your door key?" he asked her anxiously. "Don't come in too quietly, will you. Bang about a bit to let your mother know you're home. You know how she lies awake listening. She's got enough on her mind these days, as it is, with Jessica."

"Tell Mum not to worry about a thing," said Francie, kissing him lightly. "I'll be bringing a few boys back with me, so she'll hear us breaking the windows."

19

Francie hoped the party would be somewhere exotic, like on the housing estate in Battersea where the Rude Boys hung out, but it wasn't, it was just around the corner, in a respectable tree-lined street. Rosanna's father was able to pull up outside the house in his posh Porsche without fear of his tires being slashed as he sat there.

"Don't see us to the door," said Rosanna, jumping out quickly. "And just wait out here when you come to get us —we'll come out to *you*."

Once inside, things were more what the girls had in mind. The rooms were dark, smoky, and thumping with music, and Jed's parents were nowhere to be seen. Wherever you went, you fell over people sitting or sprawling around on the floor, smoking and drinking beer. Francie quite fancied being led astray, but cigarettes disgusted her and she hated the taste of beer. She managed to get hold of a can of lemonade shandy, which she drank with her hand over the label. For some reason she was stricken with shyness. Being good in the play meant nothing here. Here it was all what you were wearing, how you looked, who you were with. Rosanna was already with several boys who were crowding around her and no wonder. She was looking wonderful. She was wearing jeans, like Francie, but they were tighter and darker, and stopped at a point that was somehow crucial, just above the ankle. Her sloppy, stripy matelot top was falling slightly off one shoulder, and she had on a pair of huge hooped earrings, which she must have had hidden in her pocket out of sight of her father, as she certainly hadn't been wearing them in the car. Even in the earrings she looked like a beautiful boy, with wet-look gel in her short, spiky hair. Francie's own hair, which she'd brushed and brushed to get the hairspray out, hung down her back like Alice in bloody Wonderland. Rosanna saw her through the gloom and waved at her to come over. But one of the boys in Rosanna's group was Joe. Francie didn't really have anything against him anymore, but he didn't do much for her confidence, either. She stayed where she was, sipping her drink with its pathetic alcohol content. A weird smell was coming from the shadows of the room, where some Rasta friends of Jed's appeared to be having to manage with one weedy little cigarette between them. It occurred to Francie it might be dope. What a horrible smell it has, she thought with a sigh. Everyone seemed to be engaged in activities she couldn't join in. Zach and Amanda were slow-dancing in the middle of the room. A couple were already snogging away furiously in the corner. Across the other side of the room on a sofa sat Roy, deep in conversation with Isabel Archer. Francie was surprised to see her here. Apart from Jed's few Rasta friends, the party was strictly for the cast. Poor Isabel must be feeling a bit out of place, Francie thought. Especially as she was the only girl in the room wearing a dress. A black slinky dress with a low-cut neck—she couldn't have looked more wrong. Her blond hair was pulled back tightly from her smooth, intelligent brow. Roy was looking as though the alcoholic content of *his* drink was working all right. It had to be an optical illusion, but from where Francie stood, he appeared to have his hand on Isabel's knee.

"Want to dance?"

It was Jed, shouting at her over the music, which had just been changed to something louder and faster. Francie was flattered. Everyone knew that Jed was a brilliant dancer. There was no danger of being expected to slow-dance with *him.*

"Okay," she said, even though Ruth, who fancied him, was watching her closely. Jed didn't really need a partner anyway, only an excuse to get up and go. The people lying about on the floor rolled over to give them space. Even the snoggers stopped what they were doing to watch. Though he didn't go so far as to take her hand, Jed did at least start off opposite Francie, who did her best to keep up, making surprisingly violent use of her mane of light brown hair. But after a minute or two he went solo, flinging himself into rhythmical contortions that would have left any white woman standing. When he took to spinning like a top on the back of his head, Francie left him to it and stepped back so that she could have the privilege of watching him like everyone else. She didn't feel shy anymore—her cheeks were flushed and she clapped and shouted in time with the beat, to keep Jed going.

"You look hot," said Richard, who must have come into the room while she was dancing. "Where's your drink?"

"Don't know," said Francie, still clapping, not taking her eyes off Jed. "Lost track of it. Doesn't matter."

"I'll get you another one," said Richard. "What did you have?"

"Something in a can," said Francie carelessly. "Tasted dreadful."

"I'll find you something," said Richard, and went away. No doubt he'd come back proudly with a can of disgusting beer. But although Jed went on dancing for ages, Richard didn't reappear. Francie got sick of waiting and went to find the bathroom. She passed Toby, who was sitting all by himself, halfway up the stairs with his hair in his eyes like an overgrown Christopher Robin. It occurred to Francie that there were worse things than being too young for this party. It was possible to be too old.

She thought better of going to the bathroom, as there was someone in there already, being sick. All those months of rehearsal had taught her one thing: to be able to hold out indefinitely for a pee.

She paused to roll up her jeans a couple of notches at the ankle, and then went downstairs again. Stepping over Toby, she was tempted to sit down beside him and cheer him up with his own good news about the television program in the summer. But a lot of loud laughter was floating up from the brightly lit kitchen below, and she was drawn on down to see what was happening.

Richard was in there with a group of the smaller boys, who were taking turns getting up on the kitchen table and doing impersonations of people in the play for the others to identify. Francie was surprised to see him spending his time with such babies. She'd forgotten for the moment that they were mostly about thirteen, the same age as she was.

"*There* you are," said Richard as she came into the room. "I looked for you but you'd disappeared."

"I thought *you'd* disappeared," said Francie, tossing her hair, a mannerism she'd picked up from herself this evening. The small boys, bored by the intrusion of a girl, went on with their game.

"I found some wine," said Richard, getting up and crossing to the sink. "Want some?"

"Okay," said Francie with a shrug. Wine was something she did quite like. She sometimes had it, watered down, at Sunday lunch.

Richard rinsed out a glass and half filled it with white wine. He glanced at Francie and then topped it up with soda and orange juice. "Buck's Fizz," he said, diplomatically making it sound twice as decadent at half strength.

"Hey, Rich!" shouted a cheeky boy who was standing on the table. "Who's this?" and launched into a wicked parody of Richard as Lord Cardigan straight to his face. Richard didn't mind. He and Francie sat down at the kitchen table to watch. Francie laughed louder than anyone when another boy grabbed a tea towel and wrapped it tightly around his shoulders. The table creaked alarmingly as he rocked from side to side, singing "Just for Me" in a mincing choirboy voice.

"Come on, Richard," chorused the boys, but he refused to climb up on the furniture, which was just as well, as his head would have hit the ceiling. "Go on, Richard," said Francie, and to please her he got to his feet and did a few turns, cramped between the stove and the fridge. Not straightforward impersonations, though. Richard changed the rules; he played the parts as though by somebody else. Captain Tuckett as performed by trendy Zach. A Rasta version of the Police Inspector, as danced by Jed. Francie nearly fell off her chair with laughter. She noticed her laugh sounded different than usual: throatier and more raucous, as though she were one of the boys. But she knew it wasn't for the boys that Richard was being so funny. It was her own unladylike laugh that was egging him on. She had no desire to have a go herself. She was a pretty deadly mimic in her own right: she could have had quite a lot of success, if she'd got up and tried. But nothing to the success she was having just sitting there laughing. All you had to be in that room full of boys, was a girl.

There was a crash of breaking glass from the hall outside, and much shouting and scuffling. The boy called Hamish staggered into the kitchen with blood pouring from a cut in his lip. The room filled with excited, ministering people, washing his face, checking if his teeth were loose, offering to take him to the hospital. Out in the hall the other boy involved in the fight was lying doubled up on the floor claiming to be kicked in the goolies. There was talk of racism and riot, but nobody really seemed to know how the fight had started. In Francie's experience, nobody ever did. She'd seen boys fighting in the playground at Dubbs, and it was never heroic or exciting, as when actors hit each other in the movies. For one thing, it was always all over in a second. There would be a wild, first-flaying moment during which both boys would appear to miss each other by miles, and then they would fall to the ground, clutched in a ludicrous embrace. Dying of their injuries one minute, they would be up on their feet, bellowing obscenities, the next. Terrified as she usually was, Francie found it hotly embarrassing. Despite the spurts of real blood, it always looked to her like bad acting.

Emily and Abigail pressed forward to fuss over Hamish. They couldn't wait to be nurses or mothers or angels. Francie backed away, her hand over her own mouth in the place where Hamish's lip was bleeding.

"He'll be all right," said Richard. "It's only a scratch." The party having moved into the kitchen, he decided the time had come to move out. Grabbing the wine bottle in one hand and Francie in the other, he led her back past the casualty scenes in the hall to the front room, where only the heaviest petters remained, lying about the floor in each other's arms.

Francie was nervous that Richard might be planning to

take up the same sort of position with her. But he made for the empty sofa, where he slouched at one end, with his feet toward her, keeping her at leg's length, which in his case was a very long way away indeed. Francie, who was expecting to have to look after her own interests, was a bit put out to find them taken care of quite so thoroughly for her. Music was playing, the lights were dimmed, and all he wanted to do was talk. He asked her about her life, her ambitions. Francie was rather disappointed by the interest he took. It made him seem more like a friend of her parents than a schoolboy. How did *she* know, at her age, if she wanted to be an actress?

"I'm not sure," she said. "I hope not. Do you?"

"No," he said laughing. "Or an actor either. Acting's a mug's game. If you've got to go into the theater, the only thing worth being is a director."

"Is it?" said Francie in surprise. Not once during the production had it occurred to her to envy Toby and Roy. But Richard really coveted their job. All the time he'd been peacocking about as Lord Cardigan, all he'd really wanted to do was get down off the stage and direct. Or write. There were scenes in the play he'd have liked to completely reconstruct. Although there wasn't much you could do about the fundamental weakness of the plot.

Francie wasn't at all sure that she approved of the play's being criticized. She certainly wouldn't have stood for any of that sort of talk from her father. But she liked watching the animation in Richard's face as he spoke. She nodded or shook her head from time to time, so that his mouth would go on moving in that wriggly, witty way. According to him, the theater was on the blink anyway. What really interested him was directing films. But then the English film industry came in for some flak. The directors Richard really seemed to admire were French.

Talking of French, all the kissing going on around them

was beginning to inflame Francie's senses. The wine she was drinking now was neat, and she was feeling a bit wild and abandoned. She kicked off her shoes and arched her body backward, flicking her hair from underneath so that it spread out across the back of the sofa. Richard leaned forward, but only to top up her glass. He was naming names now—Resnais ("Sorry, who?") and Godard ("Oh, him") and some old thing that was nothing to do with pop music, called the New Wave. Francie was all at sea. She couldn't imagine what could be in it for Richard, raving on to some ignorant fourth-former when there were brainboxes of his own age at the party such as Isabel Archer, who could have thrown in a few intellectual pointers of her own. And looking the way *she* did in her black dress, talking wasn't all he'd want to do with *her.*

"Sorry," said Richard, "I'm going on. Tell me about your family. Have you got any brothers?"

"I've got a sister," said Francie. "She's about the same age as you."

"That's funny," said Richard. "My sister's more your age. Thirteen last September."

"Actually I'll be fourteen next month," said Francie, but she knew now it was hopeless. To be identified with his kid sister! No wonder he was keeping his distance. She sighed and looked at her watch. "I'm being picked up soon," she said, to set the seal on her babyishness once and for all. "Rosanna's father's coming. I suppose I'd better try and find her. I haven't seen her since we first arrived."

"She's over there," said Richard with a tilt of his head.

"*Is* she?" said Francie in surprise. Nobody had come into the room. She looked around, able to see better now that her eyes had got used to the dark. And sure enough, Rosanna had been there all the time, over in the corner on some cushions, one of the more ardent lovers, in the arms of none other than Joe.

"Oh," said Francie in embarrassment, and then got the giggles.

"What's so funny?" said Richard.

"She told me she didn't like him," said Francie, blushing to think that Rosanna could have said the same of her. She held out her glass for more wine. So much for Joe being so "obvious." There were high hopes of Rosanna proving conventional yet. "At least they're nowhere near the lavatories," she murmured, and then hoped her little joke would be lost on Richard. But he gave her one of his measured, sidelong looks. No doubt all sorts of stories about her were floating around. He'd probably heard that she was the sort of girl who screamed the place down if you laid a finger on her.

"I'm really looking forward to this thing in the summer, aren't you?" she said, to change the subject. "I mean fancy doing the play on television! It's great to think it's not all over after all."

Funnily enough, this line of coversation drew a blank with Richard. Suddenly, he could barely be bothered to be civil, let alone chat. He shifted morosely in his corner and looked away. No doubt he had better things to do than a school play when it came to the summer. Perhaps he was off to France to direct a film.

"Have you seen Toby tonight?" he said abruptly.

"Here at the party do you mean?" said Francie. "Actually I nearly fell over him before, on the stairs. I think he's sadder than anyone that tonight's the last night. I'm not nearly as upset as I thought I would be, are you? Now that I know I'll be playing Amelia again . . ."

Francie stopped speaking, at a loss to understand the aphrodisiac effect of what she had just said. For without warning, Richard had swung his legs around and moved right up close to her on the sofa. He seemed annoyed and affectionate both at once. Some of her hair had got caught behind his back. She shifted her head slightly, to convey politely that she was trapped, and he freed her at once, running the light brown strands idly through his fingers. Because her hair was long, the sensation was faint and far-off, and yet it seemed to have repercussions right through her body, as though he were touching her intimately by radar.

"My hair's greasy," she murmured. "It needs washing." But he didn't seem to hear her, and a moment later he did something that made her quite speechless. Sliding down in his seat so that his head was on a level with hers, he drew a handful of her hair over his nose and mouth and sort of breathed it, grease and all, as if his lungs depended on its all too human smell.

Francie felt like a mermaid floating over him: a soft, trancelike lassitude came over her limbs. He could kiss her now, if he wanted to. But as he turned toward her, pushing her hair out of both of their eyes, an odd, guilty expression clouded his face for a moment. He seemed about to speak, and then to change his mind. Francie's old distrust of him suddenly flooded back, and the words she'd repeated so often to herself sprang into her mind like a warning: *He tried to stop me getting Amelia.* As his face came close to hers she stiffened, and then, of course, the moment was lost. Unlike Joe, Richard would never, *never* kiss a girl who didn't want him to. That was the one thing Francie had got right on the very first day. He was, as she had snap-judged him to be, incurably proud.

He drew back and the scene was abruptly over: the doorbell rang and people came into the room, calling her name. Apparently Rosanna's father had arrived, and had come to the door as Rosanna had expressly told him not to. Rosanna was standing over her with freshly applied lipstick, nagging her to come quickly.

"Give us your phone number," people pleaded as she

was leaving, although they never really intended to ring her up. Richard didn't ask for her number, but gave her his, pressing a bit of paper roughly into her hand.

"Ring me," he said urgently, "if you've got any . . . problems between now and July. Anything you want to discuss. About the play, I mean."

About the play. So he was determined, after all, to keep things on a professional footing.

July was a long way off. Francie had more immediate problems. Such as how to walk reasonably steadily to the door. How not to throw up all over the elegant upholstery of Rosanna's father's car.

"Pissed but not kissed!" she sang, and she and Rosanna rolled around on the backseat of the car all the way home, as though it was hysterically funny.

20

Jessica's A levels loomed. Her relationship with Matthew had reached crisis point. Should she try to subdue her sexual desires until after her exams were over? Would Matthew be prepared to wait much longer? To Do It or not to Do It: which would ruin her concentration more? Personally, Francie thought they should go ahead and get It over. If Jessica was having to go around feeling anything like *she'd* felt when Richard had nearly kissed her, she didn't see how her sister's brain could be functioning properly at all. Now that Jessica had taken to bringing Matthew back to the house, she didn't get much studying done anyway. They would be upstairs in her room, Not Doing It for hours, only to emerge red-faced and more tormented than ever. But Jessica told Francie that she was superstitious. If she succumbed before her exams, she was bound to fail. Francie worried that the bargain might work both ways. Would passing with flying colors mean lifelong virginity?

It was only natural that Francie's parents should be completely taken up with Jessica's problems again. Francie was quite happy to fall back into her old habit of blending into the background. For one thing she had exams of her own. If she kept a low enough profile, it was just possible her parents wouldn't notice how much her work had slipped behind because of the play. But now that she was fourteen, blending into the background wasn't as easy as it had been. For one thing, she was bigger. She seemed to be in everyone's way. Her voice was too loud, she dropped things. People got irritated with her, even when she was keeping perfectly quiet and still.

"Get your feet off the sofa!" her mother would shout. "Must you lie around like that all day?"

The truth was that Francie felt tired. She couldn't be bothered to do anything in her spare time except flake out in her dressing gown in front of old French movies recorded off late-night television.

"What a layabout you're becoming," said her father, having watched the same film himself the night before, when she was in bed. "For God's sake, Frances, put some clothes on."

And then, of course, when she did get dressed, they started on about her appearance.

"What *is* that child wearing? And what has she got on her face? Really, Francie, I don't know what you think you look like. You're not in a play now, you know."

Lately Francie *had* been thinking rather a lot about clothes. Not that she had any money to buy any. Nearly all her pocket money went on creams and lotions for her complexion. Also she'd become a bit obsessed with the hairs on her legs. Since she'd waxed them with Rosanna they seemed to have grown back thicker. She bought some stuff from the chemist, but it stained the towels and filled the bathroom with weird fumes that got up everybody's nose.

"How can you be so absurd?" said her mother, who didn't seem to mind when the hairs on her own legs poked through her tights. "If you spent as much time on your homework as you do gazing in the mirror, there might be some hope for you at school."

It wasn't all roses there, either. Francie had imagined it would be calming to be back in the exclusive company of girls. She'd forgotten how turbulent female relationships could be. Now that there were no more Friday rehearsals, Amanda was her best friend again. Francie knew better than to go on too much about the television production in the summer. But Sarah, who had preferred having Amanda to herself, was always drawing attention to it. She referred to Francie as "our media person." She also had a way of annoying Amanda by making Francie stand up for Rosanna.

"Rosanna must be awfully worried about AIDS," she said, "with her father the way he is."

"Rosanna's father only has one partner," said Francie fiercely. "He's as good as married."

But in fact she didn't know if this was true. Privately she worried a lot about Rosanna's father. And Jessica and Matthew. And herself when she grew up.

"I'm not so keen on getting older as I used to be," she said in confidence to Jessica. "It must be awful to be your age. You and Matthew must worry about it all the time."

"We've got Mum to worry for us," said Jessica cheerfully. "She's changed her tune entirely about sex. She's not a believer in Experience anymore. She thinks Matthew and I should 'wait.' I told her I was already on the Pill in case we couldn't. 'What good is the Pill?' she shrieked. 'What you need is a sheath!' I mean of all old-fashioned words. It doesn't seem to have occurred to her that Matthew hasn't Done It with anyone before, any more than I have."

"Hasn't he?" said Francie in amazement. The innocence of Jessica's generation took her breath away. Even if Matthew was lying. "You'd better go on taking the Pill as well," she said nervously. "I'm too young to be an aunt."

"Don't worry," said Jessica. "I'm not getting pregnant just to satisfy Mum. I'm sure that's what she'd really like me to do. Then I'd have to get married to Matthew, and neither of us would be allowed to sleep with anyone else ever again."

"Where would you live?" said Francie, glancing in horror around Jessica's chaotic bedroom. "How would you do your homework?"

"Don't get *too* fussed about all this AIDS stuff," said Jessica. "I'm going to be a doctor, aren't I? I'll have it all sorted out by the time you're old enough to care."

"Get on with your studying, then," said Francie. "You may be needed sooner than you think."

Crossing the sixth-form lawn on an errand for one of her teachers, Francie ran into Isabel Archer. Francie wasn't sure whether to stop and speak to her. At Dubbs she'd always been perfectly relaxed and friendly, but here she was a prefect, and prefects had a license to be withering. But today Isabel made a special point of coming up to Francie and asking how she was getting on in her exams.

"Dreadfully," said Francie, pulling a face. "We had math today. But what about your A levels? They're miles more important. They're what you gave up the play for."

"I've only done two English papers so far," said Isabel. "They went a bit too well for comfort. I'm hoping for C's so I won't get into university. Then my parents will *have* to let me try out for drama school." She laughed, but Francie had the feeling she wanted her to know that she wasn't joking, and that the situation was causing her a lot of distress. The sun, which had a way of shining on the sixth-form lawn when the rest of the playground was in shadow, lit her blond hair like a halo. Isabel was the only person Francie could think of who actually looked good in bottle green.

"Well, good luck," said Francie awkwardly. "Or bad luck, whichever it is you want."

"I'll probably get what I deserve," said Isabel ruefully.

Francie's exams were over long before the A levels were finished, but the strain on her nerves continued until the last of Jessica's exams had been sat. After her final biology paper, Jessica stayed out late celebrating, and Francie waited up for her to come home. To pass the time she had got into Jessica's unmade bed to read, and was just dropping off when her sister came into the room.

"Well," said Francie excitedly, sitting up with the covers held under her chin. "How did it go?"

"What are you doing in *my* bed?" said Jessica.

"Waiting to see how you got on," said Francie impatiently.

"Oh, God," said Jessica, kicking off her shoes. "How can *I* tell how it went? It *felt* dreadful."

"Did it?" said Francie in alarm, although looking at Jessica it was hard to believe. Her eyes were shining and the furrow in her forehead was completely smoothed away.

"Absolutely foul," she said, leaving a trail of clothes all over the floor as she undressed. Jessica had a brilliant figure. Francie looked at her neck and shoulders for telltale marks, but there were none. "Mind you," went on Jessica, "it wasn't quite as bad as physics. At least I was able to do the multiple choice."

"I'm not talking about *biology*," said Francie in relief. "I'm talking about what you did with Matthew after it was over. Your 'celebration'! What you and Matthew have been waiting all this time to Do!"

"Oh, *That*," said Jessica with her head inside her nightie. "We did *That* ages ago."

"When?" cried Francie in high indignation. She would have asked, Where? as well, but she had a nasty feeling that it might have been here in this very bed, where she was sitting.

Jessica's face appeared, rather pinker than before, through the neck of her nightdress. "I don't remember exactly," she lied. "When Mum started warning me off, I suppose. As soon as we thought we mustn't, we couldn't help it."

"You are a cheat," said Francie admiringly. "Don't blame me if you fail your bloody exams." Secretly she had to admit she was thrilled that love had been prepared to risk all.

"So what's it like?" she said. "Going to bed together and everything."

"The going to bed was quite ordinary," said Jessica. "But the and everything was brilliant. Now get lost, Goldilocks, and let me get some sleep."

But Francie refused to budge. "Not until you tell me what it's like," she said. She had a sudden unexpected memory of Richard leaning against the bus shelter, eyeing her under his spiky lashes. "Describe it to me," she said, "in gory detail."

But Jessica, so learned in the intricate workings of the human body, proved to be a complete washout when it came to describing the act of love. The best she could come up with were expressions like "really great" and "really fantastic." Love seemed to have turned her steely intellect to mush. It wasn't that she was unwilling to talk. She sat at the foot of the bed with her knees hugged up inside her nightie, and bored away for England. But what she wanted to talk about was not sex, but Matthew. She wanted to tell Francie how wonderful he was, how winning in his ways. Once she got on to the subject you couldn't get her off it. Francie tried to steer the conversation onto other topics, such as the biology exam, but Jessica had a genius for relating everything back to Matthew. Francie yawned. She liked Matthew, but she'd seen quite a lot of him lately and had formed her own opinion of his good and bad points. She wriggled down under the bed covers and rested her head on the pillow. But late as it was, she stayed awake, flattered that her sister was prepared to confide such things to her. She wondered what Jessica would think of her own recent experiences: kissed by Joe when she didn't want to be; not kissed by Richard when she did. Nothing on God's earth would induce *her* to tell.

Jessica's exam results wouldn't be known until August: Francie's came out the following week. They were bad. Francie didn't care. She'd made a pact with God that the worse her results were, the better her sister's would be. Things were looking good for Jessica. Francie had failed math and was likely to be put down a division. She'd done well in art, but then she always had done, having picked up so much, including talent, from her parents. The rest were all very mediocre, bare fifty percent passes, with one surprising exception. She'd done much better than usual in French. It must have been all those old movies she'd been watching. But that didn't make up for the fact that her marks overall had taken a dive. Her parents' case was proved. Being in the play had had a shocking effect on her work.

Choruses of I-told-you-so aside, there wasn't a lot her parents could do about it now. The television performance was in the holidays, so they couldn't take *that* away from her. Of course, they were bound to close down on her from now on: there would be no acting *next* year if they could help it. But next year was next year. Ahead of her stretched the summer, and the chance to play Amelia one more time. And for posterity, too; they were all going to be given a video of the show to keep forever—she would be able to flake out on the sofa for years to come in front of her memories. There was the reunion with the cast to look forward to. And seeing Richard. This time she was determined to look at him in real life with the same womanly eyes as she did on the stage, as Amelia. But unlike Amelia, she wasn't so sure she would spurn him.

Francie locked herself in the bathroom and belted her way through all the numbers in the show at the top of her lungs. It was going to take more than a few bad marks to get *her* down.

"It's a matter of honor," she sang,

"When a man feels defamed
He can hardly be blamed
For shooting the other chap straight
through the heart . . ."

21

When the blow fell, it came so completely out of the blue that it seemed to cut time clean in half: into the Time Before it happened, and the Time Afterward. For a while Francie found it hard to put the two halves back together again. Sometimes, particularly when she first woke up in the mornings, she existed in a strange, vague dreamworld, where everything was still perfectly all right. And then it would come over her, the cloud of what had happened, and in that dark fog it would be impossible to remember how bright and clear the world had seemed before the phone rang.

Francie was stretched out on the sofa watching a film called *Le Boucher*, when she heard it ringing. The plot was getting really exciting: the butcher was just about to attack the schoolmistress with a meat-ax, so Francie didn't bother to get up. The phone was nearly always for Jessica anyway.

But a moment later she heard Jessica shouting her

name. So with the push of a button she put the film and her whole carefree existence on "pause," and went to pick up the receiver.

"Hello," said a voice. "It's Toby."

Francie's heart missed a beat, but only from excitement. He was ringing with the television date and rehearsal time. He sounded rather rushed.

"Oh, and by the way," he said (by the way!), "now that Isabel's exams are over she'll be coming back into the cast. So obviously, in the television version, she'll be playing Amelia."

He went on quickly to explain what Francie would be playing: everything under the sun, apparently—an Officer's Wife, a Person of Putney, a Member of the Crowd, and so on. Unfortunately, it was too late now to put her back into her original part of Mrs. Cunningham. They would need all the rehearsal time available for Isabel and a couple of replacements for boys who were going away on holiday. He didn't want to disrupt the cast any more than he had to. But Francie was not to worry. She would be on in almost every scene—more, in fact, than she had been as Amelia. And her voice would be so useful in the chorus. Some of the numbers had been sounding very thin. Francie's contribution would make all the difference.

There was a silence in which Francie was expected to speak. She said nothing.

"Don't take it personally," went on Toby. "You were wonderful as Amelia, everyone thought so. But these adjustments have to be made for the sake of the show. Television is different from the stage. It's important that Amelia should look the right age. You were a bit on the young side, you said so yourself. Remember what we said, way back at the beginning, about there being no stars, everyone pulling together like a team? Well, that still holds good. It's the play that matters, after all, isn't it. So see you in a fortnight, Okay?"

"Okay," said Francie dully, and hung up.

She went back into the living room and turned on the video again. She sat down in front of the film, but the plot no longer made sense to her. The butcher could have hacked the schoolmistress up into cutlets for all she cared. Ten minutes later she was sitting there, staring at the credits, when her mother came into the room.

"Now that's over perhaps we can have some light in here," she said, drawing back the curtains and letting the sun stream through the windows. "What a way to start your holidays, sitting in here in the dark on such a beautiful day. You ought to be outside, getting some fresh air. You're looking awfully pale. Actually, Francie, are you sure you're feeling all right?"

And then Francie began to cry.

It wasn't like crying over Bat. Her grief for him had been an innocent, healthy emotion, compared with what she was feeling now. Now her emotions turned in on her and sickened her like poison: shame and humiliation for herself, anger with Toby, hatred and jealousy of Isabel. She flung herself facedown on the sofa and buried her head in a cushion. How could she face the rest of the cast having lost her part? Emily and Ruth would be secretly triumphant. Joe would have a field day when he heard. And as for Richard . . . She kicked the arm of the sofa violently with her bare feet. Richard had been right all along. She never *had* been good enough from the beginning. It wasn't just the future that was ruined, but the past as well. She imagined them all whispering what a failure she was. She wished now that she'd never played Amelia. "I can't bear it," she moaned into the cushion. "I'll never be able to bear it."

At moments like this, Francie's family came into their

152 | MEREDITH DANEMAN

own. Her father and Jessica came running, and within seconds they were kneeling around her with her mother, protecting her on three sides, demanding to know what had harmed her.

"They don't want me to play Amelia anymore," Francie managed to get out, and although, even as she said it, she knew it was a little thing, of no worldly importance, they didn't think so; they were shattered for her, outraged on her account, prepared to fight for her cause.

"How dare they do that to you," shouted her father, "when you were so good!"

"There must be some mistake," said her mother. "I'm sure if they knew how upset you were, they'd give you back the part."

"I don't want it back," sobbed Francie. "I'd be too embarrassed to play it now. I doubt if I could even walk onto the stage."

"Well, you won't have to," said Jessica angrily. "Tell them to stuff their boring play. They can't expect you to come on in some piddling little part when you've been used to playing the lead."

Francie groaned and covered her face with her hands. She knew already that if there was one thing more shaming than not playing Amelia, it would be not to turn up at all. "I'll have to do it," she said hopelessly. All she wanted now was to be left alone. But her family was in full swing. Her father was threatening to hit Toby, Jessica to throttle Isabel. The days of dueling were obviously not dead yet.

"Don't worry," Francie said to shut them up, "I'll sort it out for myself. Maybe I'll ring Roy. He was always more on my side than Toby was." But then she remembered Roy at the last night party, thick as thieves with Isabel, and her heart sank. Recasting Amelia was probably his idea.

In the end she rang Rosanna, but *she* was no comfort.

She didn't seem to understand what Francie was making such a fuss about. She seemed to have swallowed the team-spirit propaganda hook, line, and sinker.

"What does it matter," she said, "as long as you're in it? You can't blame Isabel for wanting to come back. It doesn't matter who plays what. Anyway you'll have lots to do. You'll be really good as a Person of Putney."

"I am one already," said Francie.

"Oh," said Rosanna, who hadn't noticed. "Well, it's fun being an Officer's Wife."

"Then why doesn't Isabel be one?" said Francie stubbornly, although she knew that from Rosanna's point of view she was sounding horribly conceited. A prefect could hardly be expected to play second fiddle to a fourth-former. It had been Isabel's part in the beginning, after all. But Francie hadn't copied what she'd done. She'd made a new Amelia of her own. And now she felt the character was part of her.

"I'm afraid when I hear Amelia's cues I'll start saying her lines automatically," she said in a low voice. "I might even burst into song by mistake." But she was dramatizing when she said that. She was too heavyhearted to imagine ever singing again.

For the rest of the day Francie paced about the house, going over and over in her mind what Toby had said on the telephone. Why had she not spoken up to him? Why hadn't she said, No Toby, it's not okay, instead of just dumbly agreeing? She made up her mind to ring him back, and carried his number around with her, lifting the receiver from time to time and then putting it down again. She tried writing out a conversation in advance. *Hello, Toby,* she wrote on little scraps of paper all over the house. *It's Francie. I just wanted to say . . .*

But in the end she didn't ring. Toby and Roy were always encouraging you to speak up. Express yourself, feel equal, call them by their Christian names. But when it came to the crunch, they were teachers. They would slap you down like a child.

That evening Jessica burst in, late for dinner as usual, with some rather ironic news.

"Well!" she said. "I've just come from Isabel's house, and guess what? It's only her godfather at the BBC who's set the whole thing up! They wouldn't be putting it on at all if she wasn't playing Amelia. Naturally, Toby and Roy are prepared to go along with anything to get their precious play on television. So you see, it's no reflection on you at all, Francie."

Francie felt a rush of relief, but her mother looked stricken.

"It's all my fault," she said with her head in her hands. "I told Isabel to contact her godfather."

"Nonsense," said Francie's father angrily, "Toby and Roy are to blame. They must have known all along that this was going to happen."

"They did," said Jessica. "That's the dreadful thing. They made an agreement with Isabel way back at the beginning, that if the television thing worked out, she would have her part back. They were planning to drop Francie even before they auditioned her. Isabel says she wanted to say something ages ago. She felt terrible about it, Francie being my sister and everything. But Toby and Roy didn't want Francie told. They thought it might affect her performance. Take away her confidence."

"Heaven forbid," said Francie's father caustically.

But Francie, who hadn't touched her food up till now, was suddenly able to get down a few mouthfuls. Losing the part didn't necessarily mean she hadn't been good enough. There were politics involved here that had nothing to do with merit. Toby and Roy were no longer their own bosses. She felt sorry for them, being pushed around by Godfathers. But what was better for her, seemed worse, somehow, for the world. She sighed, and pushed away her plate again.

Her mother glanced around the table and smiled extra brightly. "I think it's time we got a new dog," she said.

22

Francie's mother seemed to think that getting a new dog was the answer to everything. Francie didn't agree. The more depressed she felt, the more she couldn't bear to contemplate the idea of a replacement for Bat. She thought it heartless of her mother to suggest such a thing, and became ruder and ruder to her every time she brought the subject up. Relations between them got so bad that when Francie got the first faint signs of the curse, accompanied by a horrid dragging ache in her stomach, she didn't tell her mother anything about it, but simply raided Jessica's cupboard for some equipment and locked herself in her bedroom. No doubt if she *had* mentioned it, her mother would have recommended a visit to Battersea Dogs' Home over and above a couple of aspirin.

Francie made sure she didn't run into Jessica. If there was one thing worse at the moment than the thought of her mother being sisterly, it was the thought of her sister being motherly. Besides, Jessica kept trying to push

Francie into coming with her to Isabel's house so that they could talk things over. Francie had nothing to say. She didn't really blame Isabel anymore, but she remembered her treacherous kiss on the first night, her patronizing manner in the playground. She didn't want to see things from Isabel's point of view. She was having enough trouble seeing them from her own.

Funnily enough, the one person Francie found she *could* talk to at the moment was her father. Not that she was prepared to tell him about the curse. But he did seem to understand better than the others how she felt about the play. He let her come up into his studio when he was working, and wander around among his expensive equipment without shouting at her every second not to knock things over.

She had always loved this room, with its magic enlarging and projecting machines, its tilting easels, and its jars full of smooth-tipped sable brushes bunched together like flowers. There was a wooden lay figure with flexible joints in one corner, which she had always longed to be allowed to dress up. At the moment it was wearing a soldier's trench coat, spattered with mud.

She stood looking over her father's shoulder as he shaded in hundreds and thousands of pebbles on a beach scene, with a scratchy nib.

"I didn't realize until I lost it," she said, "how good it made me feel to be playing Amelia. I suppose I must have been a bit conceited about it. There are people at Dubbs who'll be pleased to see me brought down. I don't thing I'll do this television thing. I honestly don't think I can face it."

"Don't, then," said her father, not looking up. "Nobody's making you."

"I know," said Francie, "but Toby said they needed me.

And the stupid thing is, even now, I'll feel as though I'm letting them down."

"It's they who've let you down," said her father, frowning as he dipped his pen in the black ink. "I hope you realize, Francie, that you were something really special in that play."

"Oh, I do," said Francie carelessly. "I was something so special they had to get rid of me in case I showed everyone else up."

"Shut up and listen to what I'm saying," said her father crossly, but she liked his crossness for once: it warmed her heart. "I know I was dead against it in the beginning, but when I saw you on the stage I had to eat my words. You could probably be a proper actress if you wanted to be. And you know I wouldn't say that lightly. There's something about you that makes people sit up and listen. Even old cynics like me. Hard to say what, really. Nothing to do with beauty, or having a wonderful voice. Just something about the way you look and move and sound that touches a chord."

Francie crossed the room and sat down on a leather chair that swiveled.

"You're just saying that," she said, swiveling away from him, "because you're my father."

"Not at all," he said sharply. "I'm an artist—I've been trained to look at things objectively. I'm speaking as a member of the audience, and I'm telling you that you've got a face that reads. People can tell immediately what you're thinking and feeling. It's surprisingly rare. Speaking as your *father*, I'd prefer you not to know such things about yourself. I'd prefer you to have nothing more to do with acting ever again."

"You needn't worry," said Francie, doing a full spin back to face him. "This business of losing my part has put me off the theater completely. You were right when you said what a rat race it was. And look at my schoolwork. It's a disaster. I wish I'd never done the play. It wasn't worth it."

But her father didn't seem to enjoy having won his point.

"Don't judge it all on this one experience," he said anxiously. "Perhaps you could be in a play at your own school next year. Jessica tells me they're planning to put on *Hamlet*—"

"No thanks," interrupted Francie, pulling a face. All-girl productions were no longer to her taste. "I'll probably end up being an artist like you. At least you can get on with it on your own, without having to rely on what other people think."

"Don't you believe it," said her father, but she could tell he was pleased.

"The trouble is I don't really know *what* I want," she went on, before he could get too excited about her following in his footsteps. "That's why I can't blame Isabel for taking my part away. She's got her heart set on acting. She's got to take any chance she can get." She picked up a pad and pencil from the table beside her and began to do a bit of idle drawing as she talked. "Actually, I'm not sure whose fault it is anymore. You can't really blame Toby and Roy either. It's natural enough for them to want to get their play on television."

Her father looked up from his work.

"They should have told you Isabel was coming back," he said categorically. "Or not given you the part in the first place."

"Oh, I don't know," said Francie, concentrating on her sketch. She was drawing the corner of the room with the lay figure dressed up as a soldier. But instead of the muddy trench coat, she was putting him in Victorian uniform. "Let's face it, I would have wanted to do it, even if

I'd known what was in store for me. And if they *had* told me I was only a stand-in, it *wouldn't* have been the same. I would always have felt under Isabel's shadow. I'd never have come to think of myself as Amelia. Let alone Amelia as me."

But her father wouldn't listen to excuses.

"All this wanting the best for the play is all very well. But if you ask me, those two are a bit too interested in their own glory. They ought to try to remember the purpose of the exercise. It's *children* they're dealing with in case they've forgotten . . ."

Francie drew a flamboyant moustache on her soldier. He was beginning to take on an unnerving look of Richard.

"You're too young," her father was grumbling, "to be messed around like that. It's not fair to leave you in the dark without explaining . . ."

Francie's father's words echoed in her ears. The soldier's face stared up at her from the page. *Too young. Not fair.* The words Richard had used against her at the audition. The self-same words her father was using now in passionate defense of her honor.

A blush ran through her body like a flame. The shame was so strong, it almost made her laugh. How could she have been so mistaken? Richard had been on her side all the time. It seemed so obvious, once she realized it, it was as though she had known it all along. And yet, knowing it changed everything.

She ripped her sketch off the pad and tore it into little pieces before her father could see it and start criticizing the perspective. But he was still banging on about the play.

"I'm sure no one would blame you," he was saying, "if you decided to opt out of this television fiasco. I mean there's no need to put yourself through it if you don't feel up to it. We could all go away somewhere together if you liked. I was planning a trip to Cornwall later in the holidays anyway. Your mother could do with a break, and Jessica might prefer to go earlier—"

"It's all right, Dad," said Francie, getting to her feet. "I've made up my mind to do it. I'd like to go back to Dubbs, one last time. I've got some good friends there. People I want to see again."

"All right," said her father gently. "But tell me if there's anything I can do. I don't like to see my little girl so pale and depressed."

"Actually, there is one thing that might cheer me up," said Francie suddenly.

"Anything."

"I'd like to have my hair cut."

Her father's face fell. "What, all off?" he said sorrowfully.

"Yep," said Francie firmly. "You see, they made me keep it long for Amelia. Cutting it off would make me stop wishing. It'd be like telling them they couldn't have me anymore, even if they wanted me."

Her father hooted with approval. "Have it on me," he said eagerly, fishing in his pocket for some money, prepared to see her childhood swept away at a stroke, if it made way for an independent spirit.

23

The people from the BBC invaded Dubbs like an army. They swarmed all over the place with their lights and cameras and sound equipment, smoking and swearing and swilling black coffee out of plastic cups. The technicalities that kept the film crew so busy bored the cast to death. There was nothing to do but stand about waiting, while the director and the lighting man argued about camera positions and the sound men dragged wires across the stage under their feet where they were supposed to dance. Toby and Roy stood by helplessly, as vital bits of scenery were dismantled and moved out of the way to improve the camera angles. Just when the actors were falling asleep on their feet, Isabel's godfather would suddenly snap his fingers at them and they would be expected to burst into excited action.

Each little section had to be done again and again. And the scenes were not even played in the proper order. The street scenes, for instance, all had to be shot one after another, regardless of the story. It was impossible to get into the spirit of the play, let alone inside the skin of a character. Not that Francie had any character to portray. She just kept changing her costume from rags to riches and doing whatever came next. Nobody bothered to rehearse her. They were too busy concentrating on Isabel and the principals. Toby had taken one look at her new hairstyle and clapped her into a large, elaborate poke bonnet, inside which, to her great relief, her face could hardly be seen. When she did have to take it off, it was only to pull a ragged blanket over her head, so she managed to keep her feelings pretty well under cover. But in fact it was all rather less painful than she had expected. For one thing, it turned out that they weren't actually doing the whole play—only a potted version of it. What had lasted the best part of two hours had been broken down to a bare forty-five minutes. And there was no audience, although they had to *pretend* there was. "Don't worry," said the Godfather reassuringly. "We'll be dubbing in the audience reaction later." Francie found pretending to be applauded strangely immoral. Having no audience was like finding an important member of the cast completely missing. It was like hitting a ball over a net with no one to bat it back. It was hard to be jealous of Isabel under such trying circumstances.

Funnily enough, if she was jealous of anyone, it was of Abigail, playing Mrs. Cunningham. The part of Amelia now seemed beyond her reach, out of her league: it was as though she had never played it. But Mrs. Cunningham had once rightfully been hers. If only she'd stuck to it, she would be playing it now. It offended her to see Abigail, who could be bitchy enough in real life, going through her lines with so little understanding of the woman's mischievous nature. As an Officer's Wife, Francie had to join in the chorus of "Officers' wives lead very dull lives," only to

stand back while Abigail sang what had once been her
own solo verses, slightly off the note. At least Isabel was
good, as Amelia. You had to admit she was. When *she* wore
Francie's plain gray dress you could see Richard's point
about its simplicity. She looked virtuous and lovely in it,
despite its being a bit too tight for her around the chest.

But when it came to the singing of "Just for Me,"
Francie took it upon herself to slip away. Surely no one
would miss her. She obviously wasn't needed for the
scene, so what was the point of staying on with the others
to watch? Toby had said they would be breaking in twenty
minutes' time for lunch. She decided to have hers early.

She crept cautiously back to the dressing room. You had
to be careful: there'd been bright lights in there before,
and a man with a hand-held camera, filming people as
they got their makeup on. But there was no one in sight
now. Even the wardrobe women had disappeared.

Francie took off her bonnet and ran her fingers roughly
through her hair. It still felt new and surprising to her. It
had caused quite a hit when she'd arrived at rehearsal
yesterday. People had been able to make teasing personal
remarks about it, instead of not knowing what to say to
her in her embarrassing predicament. "You look brilliant," the girls had said, and the boys had claimed to be
grief-stricken. It had all been rather gratifying, even
though they were probably lying.

The strains of "Just for Me" were reaching the dressing
room, so without bothering to take off the rest of her
costume (she had got to wear one of the striped, silky
dresses at last), Francie took her lunch box and went out
into the playground. It had been a beautiful morning, but
now a wind had sprung up and the sun kept disappearing
temporarily behind the gathering clouds. Francie found a
sheltered patch of grass under a tree and sat down and
unwrapped her sandwiches. She was surprised how hun-

gry she was. The branches spread over her and her wide Victorian skirts spread around her. She felt rather peaceful and remote from the circus going on inside the school. The sandwiches were tuna fish: her favorite. She munched away steadily, thinking of Richard and the way he had pointedly left his place in the middle of the stage whenever there was a break in the action to come over and laugh and joke with her, a mere member of the chorus. Whereas Joe, of course, had been all over Isabel. It must be galling for Rosanna to watch him shamelessly chatting up the director's godchild.

A little band of film people emerged from the school building and made their way down the stone steps: three male members of the crew, lugging a lot of equipment, and a journalist whom Francie had seen before, on television. They spotted Francie under the tree and made their way toward her.

"May we join you?" asked the journalist politely, smiling down at Francie with her back toward the sun.

"Of course," said Francie, feeling a bit embarrassed. If they were hoping for some of her sandwiches, they were out of luck: she had just bitten into the last one. She began to hitch at her skirts so that she could shift over a bit to make room for them with all their paraphernalia. But the cameraman said sharply, "Don't move! The light's perfect just where you are."

Francie froze with her sandwich an inch from her lips.

"Don't worry," said the woman, sitting down on the grass facing Francie. "Just carry on eating your lunch as though we weren't here. We just want to talk to you for a bit, that's all."

"You don't want to talk to *me*," said Francie in alarm. "I'm no one in the play. The others will be out in a minute."

The cameraman's assistant glanced nervously at the sky.

"Be better now," he said, holding a tape measure to her nose.

The sound man trailed his microphone over to her. "Mary had a little lamb," he said several times in a row.

The journalist ignored the men and began to chat to Francie in a cozy, girls-together sort of way.

"Don't worry about the camera," she said confidentially. "It doesn't matter what you say—we'll edit it later. We probably won't use much of it anyway." She laughed and Francie was riveted by her teeth, which were large and gray with a gap at the front. *She* obviously couldn't care less what the viewers thought of *her.* "What do you think of this acting lark?" she said. "How did you get involved in it in the first place?"

Her manner was so casual and coaxing, it was impossible not to find yourself chatting away quite freely to her after a minute or two. Anyway, Francie felt in a strangely indiscreet mood. The mad make-believe of this so-called documentary, which required you to pretend to be acting in front of an imaginary audience, had made her impatient for a few home truths. She was prepared to tell this woman what it had really been like, starting from the very beginning. She told her about the auditions at her school, her first visit to Dubbs, the games they had played in rehearsal. And the more she talked, the more her old enthusiasm came flooding back, and she remembered what fun it had been, and how glad she was, really, that she'd done it. She felt her cheeks getting hotter and hotter as she tried to describe the extraordinary bond of friendship the actors had built up with each other over the months.

"Ah, yes," said the woman, who like all good interviewers was a bit on the psychic side, "but what about the pitfalls? The intrigues, the disappointments, the jealousies?"

Francie hesitated. She felt no overwhelming loyalty toward Toby and Roy, but she didn't really want to get drawn into talking about Amelia. There were other, broader problems on her mind. The sky grayed over as she struggled to explain the side of acting that troubled her. She had thought a lot, for instance, about the way actors could only become somebody else by using anything they could lay their hands on—real feelings they'd had in different circumstances, people (or dogs) they had known. Was it all right to borrow from life like that? Neither she nor the journalist could be sure. It also worried Francie how you could so easily get muddled between what people appeared to be on stage and what they were like in real life. She and the journalist both agreed that acting, childish as it was as a pastime, might sometimes be a rather dangerous occupation for children.

Francie and the journalist were so deep in their musings that they didn't notice that the rest of the cast had gradually come out into the playground. Francie glanced up to see Abigail and Emily pulling frantic faces at her over the top of the woman's head.

"What is it?" said Francie with a sigh.

"You shouldn't be eating in your costume," said Emily in a scandalized voice. "Toby'll kill you if he catches you."

Francie picked up her apple and bit into it with a loud and satisfying crunch. But she got to her feet and introduced them to the journalist as Mrs. Cunningham and the Miller's Wife. "You can talk to them now," she said carelessly. "They've got proper parts."

The remaining afternoon's filming went rather more quickly for Francie. They were shooting the courtroom scene, and she had quite a lot of fun sitting in the public gallery for the first time, booing and cheering the mad antics of the peers. It was quite interesting to see events from a point of view other than Amelia's. She had a chance to watch Richard's performance closely, for one thing. In her opinion he was streets ahead of anyone else. The cameraman obviously thought so, too, despite having the Godfather at his elbow, encouraging him to go into close-up on Isabel. Richard had better look out if he didn't want to be an actor. He was in danger of being discovered.

It was ten o'clock at night before they finished, by which time not one member of the cast had any illusions left about filming being a glamorous job. They were all much too exhausted for any late-night company festivities. But there was to be one final get-together at the end of the holidays, when there would be a preview of the film before it went out on television in the autumn.

"Well done, everybody," said Toby. "That was a real team effort."

Team or no team, Francie looked for Richard before she left, to tell him how outstanding he had been. But he found her first and seemed to want to congratulate her instead.

"What for?" said Francie, blushing, thinking he was sending her up.

"The best performance you've probably ever given. It must have taken some acting ability to get through today with a good grace."

"I nearly didn't turn up," said Francie confidentially.

"I'm glad you did," said Richard. "Hey, I've got something for you."

He dug in the pocket of his jeans and produced a T-shaped piece of paper: a review of *An Affair of Honor* cut out of the Dubbs' School magazine. Francie couldn't help her eyes going straight to her own name, as he'd underlined the bit about her in green ink.

"Among the visiting girls," the column read, "special

mention must be made of Frances Emmerson. Although young and fragile-looking, she portrayed Amelia with great intensity and spirit. The very essence of a Victorian heroine, there was nevertheless something modern and forthright about her performance which added an extra dimension to the evening. No wonder Lord Cardigan found her irresistible!"

With Richard watching her so intently, Francie's reading got a bit dyslexic, but she got the gist of the notice in the end. "Thanks," she said with a gulp, handing it back, but he waved her hand away.

"Keep it," he said grandly. "And take better care of it than you did of my telephone number. I thought you were going to ring me."

"I will now," said Francie with sudden boldness, tossing what was left of her hair.

"That's no use," said Richard, frowning impatiently. "I'm going away next week."

"So am I," said Francie. "I was forgetting."

"Where're you going?"

"Only Cornwall. I suppose you're going to France."

"Hardly," said Richard, laughing. "I'm going to my grandmother's in Scunthorpe. I'll be back for the preview, though. Will you?"

"I expect so," said Francie. "If I can face it."

Richard's eyes went suddenly solemn. "It's probably just your hair," he said. "But you seem to have got much older since I saw you last."

"Older and wiser," said Francie softly, by way of admitting she'd misjudged him.

24

Jessica refused to come with the family to Cornwall. She wanted to wait in London for her A-level results.

"I'll stay and look after the house," she said, "in case there's a burglar."

"If there's a burglar, I'd rather you were with us," said her mother anxiously.

But Jessica was adamant. Francie suspected it wasn't just the postman she couldn't be parted from. With the family away, she and Matthew could try out all the beds in the house.

With no Bat or Jessica to fill up the car, Francie was allowed to take a friend. She chose Amanda, and it was pleasant to have her to herself, away from Sarah's clutches. The two girls lazed about on the shiny Cornish rocks, discoursing on the dangers of granite radiation and other girlish topics. The one thing they hardly discussed at all was the play. Francie suddenly found that she was as bored with the subject as Amanda was. She wasn't bored with the thought of Richard, though.

"Of course," she confided to Amanda, "it'd never work out between us. Obviously I'm miles too young for him. He'll probably be going to film school or somewhere brilliant in September. He'll meet hundreds of girls there who'll do whatever he wants. I won't even come into his mind."

"I'm sure you will," said Amanda, but she didn't sound too convinced. It was hard for her to conceive of a skinny school friend as a love object.

"Anyway," Francie went on rather tragically, "it's too late for anything to happen now. If only I hadn't wasted so much time hating him the way I did. Now that I've found out I like him, I'm never going to see him again."

"Don't dramatize, Francie," said Amanda impatiently. "You're going to this preview thing you told me about. You'll be seeing him again in a fortnight."

The hotel they were staying in was high on a cliff, overlooking the sea. Francie and Amanda spent hours and hours in the water. It was lovely to be able to swim with your head under, without being weighted down by waterlogged hair. Francie's, darker for having been cut, picked up the sun in bright stripes.

Jessica phoned through with her results. Superstition was confounded: despite jumping the gun with Matthew, she'd got a brilliant A and two B's. Her place at university was assured. Francie's father drove them down the coast to a posh restaurant, and they had a delicious meal to celebrate. Everyone toasted Jessica in her absence. "Here's to hard work!" said Francie's father, unable to resist a significant glance at his younger daughter. Francie smiled at him innocently and raised her glass. Here's to love as well, she thought to herself. Here's to everything, all at the same time.

On the way back to the hotel, Francie's parents took a sentimental detour to the bit of coastline where they'd stayed ten years ago, when Francie was little. While the grown-ups stayed on the beach paddling and building sand castles, the two girls wandered away up the dusty track which Francie had described to Roy at the very first audition. Francie wanted to show Amanda the cottage that she'd stayed in, and the identical one next door to it where she'd had the creepy experience with the two old people. But although there were several small houses at intervals along the road, not one of them looked the slightest bit like its next-door neighbor. Nor were they shabby or ramshackle as Francie had thought she remembered. They were all poshed up and glassed in and painted different colors. Each had an individual name: Seaview (?) or The Haven. But not even a four-year-old who couldn't read could possibly have made a mistake between them.

"I don't understand," said Francie, walking backward and forward in confusion. "I thought I remembered it clearly. And if the houses are so different, what about those two old people? Did I imagine the whole thing? What do you think, Amanda? Was it true or wasn't it?"

But Amanda was already agitating to get back to the beach. "Who cares if it was true or not," she said impatiently. "It was only supposed to be a story."

25

The Godfather showed them the film in a special viewing room at the BBC. The cast sat in rows in the dark, rustling their candy wrappers as though at the cinema. They weren't a very well-behaved audience. The smaller boys kept climbing over the flap-up seats into other rows and whooping every time the announcer mentioned the name of Dubbs. Roy had to get up at one stage and bellow at them as though they were at school. They were particularly restless at the beginning because the lady journalist took so long to introduce the play. Flashing her gray, gappy smile, she described the exciting new drama projects being tackled by schools; the therapy of role-playing in adolescence; the glorious unselfconsciousness of children. The children were unselfconsciously bored stiff. But they soon perked up when the play started.

Watching yourself blown up and animated on the screen was a weird experience. It was like seeing your part being played by another person. Of course, in

Francie's case her part *was* being played by another person. The Amelia she thought she knew so well had grown several inches, dyed her hair blond, and acquired a rich, mellifluous singing voice that sprang deep from an unexpected bosom. Francie had trouble catching sight of her real self at all. She was always just cropped off the side of the picture, or out of focus at the back. Not that she was able to take in much of what she was looking at anyway. For one thing, the play had been so hacked about that it was hardly recognizable. And for another, her concentration was seriously impaired by the fact that she was sitting next to Richard, who was, of all things, holding her hand.

He'd reached out for it automatically when the lights went down, the way he always had at Dubbs, before the curtain call. But the film was only just beginning and he showed no sign of letting go. It wasn't as though he was doing any of the suggestive things she'd heard boys did when they held hands, such as wiggling his thumb about in her palm, or pressing with his nail against her skin. His grip was quite natural and reassuring, as though she were a child crossing the street. But she didn't feel the least bit safe with him. She felt dangerously, thrillingly at risk.

She fixed her eyes on the screen the way she fixed them on the blackboard when her mind was elsewhere at school, and after a while she adjusted enough to this hand-holding business for a few vague impressions to filter through to her.

Impressions was certainly the word for it. They were all that were left of the play. No sooner was a scene under way than the journalist would break in to explain the story, which would have explained itself perfectly well in a moment, if the actors had been allowed to continue. The producer *would* keep cutting away to what he obviously considered more interesting: atmospheric sequences in the dressing room, archive footage of old Wimbledon, an interview with Toby in his tracksuit. Even the singing of "Just for Me" was interrupted by close-ups of Roy sweating as he waved his baton, and a sequence that showed him relaxing at the piano and giving a few tips on composing. Just let us hear the *song,* thought Francie, feeling faintly sorry, now, for Isabel. Still, as the goddaughter as well as the heroine, she did a good deal better than some people, whose best bits had been cut out completely. It was a relief in a way, for Francie, to have no best bits of her own to worry about. She worried instead about Richard, whom she hoped would be shown to advantage. But every time he appeared on the screen her stomach would turn over to think that that glowering, whiskery man up there was sitting thigh to thigh with her in the dark. She took to closing her eyes when he came on, for fear that these internal jolts of hers might shock him if they traveled down her arm and through the unbroken circuit of his hand.

But suddenly her eyes flew open with a start. She snatched her hand from Richard's and clapped it over her mouth. But nothing could stop the sound of her voice, which was coming loudly and unmistakably from the sound track, speaking words that were nothing to do with the play at all. Francie was staring into her own face, enlarged to monstrous proportions on the screen.

People in other rows twisted their heads around to look at her. She wanted quite simply to die. But her image up there in front of her was looking all too lively. It was waving its hands about and talking with its mouth full. "You think it's going to be fun," it was saying, "but it isn't, it's really hard work. And then after a while you realize the work *is* the fun."

The film cut tellingly to the Peers leaping about like dervishes, using all their energy and ingenuity to appear as brainless and arthritic as possible. But Francie couldn't relax and enjoy the rest of the film after that. She had a nasty feeling she might not have seen the last of herself.

She was relieved when the finale was over and the cast launched into the sham bowing act. You could tell by the way the actors were eyeing each other that they weren't hearing the enthusiastic applause on the sound track. And then, just as she thought she was safe, there was the other Francie again, speaking over the final chorus, filling the screen with her awful homily on acting. She was in longer shot this time, sitting under the tree in her stripy dress, her shorn, modern head poking incongruously from the frilled old-fashioned collar.

"You go over and over what you have to do," she was saying, "and it only seems to get deader and deader. And then one day"—the camera moved in close at this point— "you're on the stage and the audience is with you, and something . . . really amazing happens. You become . . . I don't know . . . another person. It's not like you're *pretending* to be someone else. It's like someone else had decided to be *you*. And yet you're still there. It's a really amazing feeling. It's worth all the bad times just for that . . ."

On the word *that*, Francie's magnified eyebrows drew together slightly as though she had second thoughts about what she was saying. And the picture froze and left her like that, half elated, half doubtful, while the credits rolled like army tanks over her nose and mouth, as well they might.

Francie could have died of the humiliation. What would they *think* of her, pushing herself into the limelight like that? Talking as if she had a right to speak in their behalf. Had she really *said* those stupid things? She must have done—the evidence was there. But she'd said them as answers to *questions*. What had happened to the journalist? Why wasn't *she* on the scene? Francie had been left looking as though she was making speeches. *How* could she have trusted that woman?

But when the lights went up, more people crowded around her than ever had when she'd played Amelia. Everyone vied with each other to tell her how brilliant she'd been.

"How could you think what to say?" they said. "I'd have been completely tongue-tied." They dismissed their own performances as mere acting. "You looked so *real*," they said, "the way you munched that sandwich . . ."

"But I *was* eating the sandwich," protested Francie uneasily. "They caught me unawares, that was all." She was beginning to form some pretty strong opinions on documentary film-making in general. She'd treat them to those as well, in a moment, if they weren't careful.

Toby didn't seem particularly put out that his play had been chopped to pieces. Like everyone else, he seemed strangely awed that it had appeared on the screen at all.

"You made some very interesting points, Frances," he said to her seriously. "I'd really like to have a proper talk to you about the theater sometime."

Francie was flattered, but she didn't think she would risk taking him up on it. Even now she still expected to be shouted at for eating in her costume.

On the way back to Dubbs in the school bus everyone wanted to sit next to her. Trapped in a three-seat between Joe and Isabel, she shot a rueful look at Richard, who was strap-hanging farther down the aisle. His body swayed indolently as the bus took a corner. She hoped he wasn't offended with her snatching her hand away like that.

"I'm so glad the film worked out so well for you," said Isabel, on her right, anxious to convey she'd had a hand in things. "I saw the rushes of the film before it was edited. I *told* my godfather the interview with you was the best thing in it."

And Joe, on her left, was offering her chewing gum again, while complimenting her on her tan, her sun-flecked hair, her taste in clothes. (Actually, the skirt and top she was wearing were Jessica's.)

"No, thanks," said Francie, aware that Richard was watching. "How were your exam results?" she asked, turning back to Isabel.

"Straight C's," said Isabel, winking. "But I've decided to compromise. You can get a degree in drama at Middlesex Poly."

Sausage rolls and soft drinks had been laid in for the cast in the old rehearsal room. "No booze, I'm afraid," said Roy, apologetically. "It wouldn't look too good on the expenses sheet." But to judge from the spectacular size of his girth, he had a few bottles tucked under his jacket for the old boys. And the younger ones got drunk on soft drinks anyway.

Francie didn't feel like eating or drinking a thing. Something strange kept happening to her appetite every time she looked at Richard.

"Come for a walk," he said suddenly, close to her ear.

As it was holiday time, the playground was empty except for a small group of boys from the cast who were idly engaged in their usual form of entertainment: hitting each other and rolling about in a scrum. But as a sixth-former and no doubt a sports captain, Richard had access to parts of the grounds she had never visited before. He took her across some playing fields to a leafy garden, where the original old Victorian schoolhouse had once stood. He walked looking straight ahead with hooded eyes, not talking at all or attempting to hold her hand. His eyelashes had been bleached even whiter by the Scunthorpe sun.

Francie felt shy, as though she didn't know him at all. For all that she was such a blabbermouth on television, here, with the person she most wanted to impress, she couldn't think of anything to say. She didn't like to ask what he was going to do, now that he was leaving Dubbs. She was afraid he would think she was making some claim on his future. So she just walked silently beside him. He was sauntering; she was walking slightly faster, since his legs were longer than hers. It was a lovely, light, warm August evening. Francie, a bit breathless, felt strangely susceptible to the beauty of nature. The grass in the old garden was long, and stroked her ankles. Midges swirled in the air like silver dust. Richard stopped and leaned against a broken wall that was pitted with moss and draped with dark, dank ivy. Something about the way his long arms hung loosely by his sides made him look oddly helpless. "I can't touch your hair anymore," he said suddenly, "without touching you as well."

He reached out and ran his hand over the crown of her head and, as she moved toward him, his fingers slid down toward the back of her neck, where her hair was growing furrily through along the hairline. She let her head fall forward against his chest and then she felt his lips on the bony knobs of her neck, and his breath causing shivers in the hot, moist places he was making.

"Beautiful girl," he murmured against her skin, and Francie had the wisdom to know, as she would not know later, when she was older and more experienced with men, that he meant all girls, everywhere, all the pretty women he had longed for in his life, and would long for later on, in years to come. And far from offending her, it filled her with ardent happiness to know that she belonged to the half of the human race that could provoke such sweet and aching generalities. She lifted her face and let her head fall backward so that he would know what she wanted him to do next. And he looked at her for a long time before he kissed her, so that she could see how seriously he wanted to.

And when he did, the feeling was so new, and wild, and unimaginable, that Francie could have sworn it was the very first time it had ever happened to her. His arms were around her neck; hers were under his arms and around his back, where his shirt had got soaked from the wet ivy leaves. "You'll get cold," she said when she could speak, leading him away from the damp wall, quite motherly and confident, now that he'd kissed her. It was in a way as if the kiss had stood between them: a barrier that was holding back their friendship.

For now Francie found she could tell him anything, without feeling the slightest bit shy, or thinking how much older than her he was. They talked about the play, and how unhappy she'd been. He'd had a big row over her with Toby and Roy.

"Why did you stand up for me?" said Francie, who would never understand it.

"I liked you," said Richard with a shrug, "from the first time I saw you."

"But I was so awful to you," said Francie, and they retraced their relationship, right from the very first rehearsal to the last night party.

"I thought you liked Joe," said Richard, and Francie shuddered at the memory of that miserable day. Suddenly she found herself telling him all about Bat.

"You mean to say he died the day before the dress rehearsal?" said Richard, who had a dog of his own and could imagine just how dreadful it must have been for her. He kissed her to show how shocked and sorry he was. But not sexually, on the lips the way Joe had. Chastely, on the forehead, as though she were his sister.

"Haven't you thought of getting a new dog," he said, "after all this time?"

"My mother keeps on about it," said Francie. "She seems to think I need one to cheer me up. But I don't want to. I'd never like it a quarter as much as Bat. And if I did, I'd feel too disloyal."

"Perhaps it's your mother who needs cheering up," said Richard shrewdly. "She's probably dreading your sister going away to university. My mother's been really depressed since she's known I'm going to Manchester."

"Maybe you're right," said Francie, feeling a bit depressed herself. "I never really thought of it from her point of view. Maybe I ought to get one after all for her sake."

"What sort would you get?" said Richard, who favored what he had himself, a border collie, and they discussed the possibilities: terriers, Labradors, setters—anything but a spaniel.

"I'll probably just go to Battersea Dogs' Home and see which one picks me," said Francie, and they kissed again, but rather fiercely this time. And afterward Richard seemed to get a bit moody and strange. Francie guessed it must be because he was leaving his dog, and Dubbs; and because Manchester, where he was going, was a long way away.

"I'll write to you," he said as they walked back across the playing fields. He'd found an old soccer ball and was dribbling it along in front of him.

"You won't," said Francie gently. "You'll have too many essays. But I'll write to you, I expect."

"We'll see who does what," said Richard, and he kicked the ball hard, and it flew and bounced and rolled away into the distance.

ABOUT THE AUTHOR

MEREDITH DANEMAN was born in Tasmania, educated in Sydney, and went to England on a scholarship to the Royal Ballet School when she was seventeen. In London she appeared with the Royal Ballet and as Helen of Troy in a production of *Dr. Faustus,* where she met her husband, the actor Paul Daneman. Returning home, she joined the Australian Ballet for a year and published a book of poems. She came back to England, married, and worked as a model, winning the *Vogue* Model Contest in 1967. Her first novel, *A Chance to Sit Down,* was published to great acclaim in 1971 and was later televised in Britain. A second novel, *The Groundling,* followed in 1982, and will be dramatized on television. *Francie and the Boys* is her first novel for children.

She has two daughters and lives in Putney, London.